Y0-BVP-936

SIGNET Books for Young Adults

- [ ] GROVER by Vera and Bill Cleaver. (#Y6714—$1.25)
- [ ] I WOULD RATHER BE A TURNIP by Vera and Bill Cleaver. (#W9539—$1.50)
- [ ] ME TOO by Vera and Bill Cleaver. (#W9593—$1.50)
- [ ] WHERE THE LILIES BLOOM by Vera and Bill Cleaver. (#W8065—$1.50)
- [ ] THE WHYS AND WHEREFORES OF LITTABELLE LEE by Vera and Bill Cleaver. (#Y7225—$1.25)
- [ ] A FIVE-COLOR BUICK AND A BLUE-EYED CAT by Phyllis Anderson Wood. (#Y9109—$1.25)
- [ ] GET A LITLE LOST, TIA by Phyllis Anderson Wood. (#J8933—$1.50)
- [ ] WIN ME AND YOU LOSE by Phyllis Anderson Wood. (#Y8028—$1.25)
- [ ] I THINK THIS IS WHERE WE CAME IN by Phyllis Anderson Wood. (#Y7753—$1.25)
- [ ] SONG OF THE SHAGGY CANARY by Phyllis Anderson Wood. (#W9793—$1.50)
- [ ] YOUR BIRD IS HERE, TOM THOMPSON by Phyllis Anderson Wood. (#Y8192—$1.25)
- [ ] FIVE WERE MISSING by Lois Duncan. (#W8678—$1.50)
- [ ] DOWN A DARK HALL by Lois Duncan. (#W9491—$1.50)*
- [ ] LAD: A DOG by Albert Payson Terhune. (#E8090—$1.75)
- [ ] LAD OF SUNNYBANK by Albert Payson Terhune. (#E9078—$1.75)

* Price slightly higher in Canada

ELLEN GRAE
and
LADY
ELLEN GRAE

by
Vera and Bill Cleaver

A SIGNET BOOK

NEW AMERICAN LIBRARY

TIMES MIRROR

Ellen Grae COPYRIGHT © 1967 BY VERA AND
WILLIAM J. CLEAVER

Lady Ellen Grae COPYRIGHT 1968 BY VERA AND
WILLIAM J. CLEAVER

 SIGNET TRADEMARK REG. U.S. PAT. OFF. AND FOREIGN COUNTRIES
REGISTERED TRADEMARK—MARCA REGISTRADA
HECHO EN CHICAGO, U.S.A.

SIGNET, SIGNET CLASSICS, MENTOR, PLUME, MERIDIAN AND NAL
BOOKS *are published by The New American Library, Inc.,
1633 Broadway, New York, New York 10019*

FIRST SIGNET PRINTING, FEBRUARY, 1978

4 5 6 7 8 9 10 11 12

PRINTED IN THE UNITED STATES OF AMERICA

ELLEN GRAE

To
Special Agent
Phoebe Larmore
With
Affection

Mrs. McGruder isn't a religious person especially, although she and Mr. McGruder attend the Methodist Church every Sunday and when I live with her I have to leave off being a Pantheist and turn Methodist too. But she likes to have people talk to her about religion.

So, wanting to please her, I told her that I had learned to be most truly, humbly grateful for all the benevolences God had seen fit to bestow upon me.

She turned a light green gaze upon me and asked, "Oh? What brought that on?"

"Nothing brought it on," I explained. "I just started feeling grateful toward Him. I feel grateful toward you, Mrs. McGruder. For letting me come back down here and stay with you while I go to school. I vow that I've changed since last year and won't be as much trouble to you this year as I was last."

She said, "Well, if that's true it'll be my turn to be grateful. Like what, for instance, have you changed?"

"Well, for one thing I take a bath every night now without anybody hollering at me to do it and for another I've stopped swearing. I don't even say hell any more. I think that the use of profanity is a vocabulary deficiency, don't you?"

"At the moment I can't think," Mrs. McGruder said, handing me a freshly sugared doughnut. "I'm too busy counting my blessings."

"I know a girl whose father, they said, dropped

dead from swearing. Her name's Opal Gridley. Her father's name was Fortis Alonzo and I think that's what killed him."

"I'm really trying but I don't get the connection," Mrs. McGruder said.

"You will in a minute. Well, anyway, he was a meter reader for the gas company and I guess that and his having a name like Fortis Alonzo burdened him heavily and made him feel unimportant."

"I think Fortis Alonzo is rather a pretty name," Mrs. McGruder murmured.

"Do you? Well, that's what it was. Fortis Alonzo Gridley. He used to drive around with all the windows in his car rolled up. Even when everybody else was standing around pouring sweat and with their tongues hanging out having trouble breathing because it was so hot, Mr. Gridley would get in his car and roll up all the windows and drive around and wave to people."

"I'm still trying," Mrs. McGruder said.

"His wife was fat and could sing Italian. She practiced every night after supper. If you listened it was sadly pretty but nobody did. They'd all come out on their porches and stand around and laugh and this made Mr. Gridley mad. He'd run out of his house and shake his fist at them and swear. When he died everybody said that's what caused it. They said God struck him dead for swearing so much. But do you know something?"

"I'm beginning to think not," Mrs. McGruder said.

"Mr. Fortis Alonzo Gridley died at his own hand. Trying to make people think he was rich enough to have an air-conditioned car. He didn't have it though and that's what killed him. The heat and no air at all. I was the one who got to him first the night he collapsed. Gridley's house was next door to ours and when I saw Mr. Gridley drive up weaving and wobbling I ran over and jerked the door of his car open and he fell out. He didn't have time to say one word. Just blew a bubble and died."

"What do you mean he blew a bubble?"

"He blew a bubble while he was dying. It looked like glass. Mrs. McGruder?"

"Yes, Ellen Grae?"

"Was that telegram that came a few minutes ago from Rosemary?"

"It was from her father. She'll be in on the ten o'clock train. Are you ready for more breakfast now?"

"No thanks. I still hate breakfast; I haven't changed that much. Will I have to room with her again?"

"That's my plan. Why?"

"Oh, nothing. It's just that I was thinking it might be better if I could have a room to myself this year. I forgot to tell you and I'll bet Grace did too that lately I have these strange seizures."

"Seizures? What kind of seizures?"

"Seizures. You know. They always come at night. I get up and crash around and cry out. I know when I'm doing it but I can't stop myself. Jeff says it's a very frightening thing to watch. He says it's almost as if I was disembodied. I was just thinking it might be better if Rosemary could be spared the sight. You know how frail she is."

"No, I hadn't noticed," Mrs. McGruder said, setting two scrambled eggs and a glass of milk in front of me. "I'll be on the lookout for one of your attacks but in the meantime could you just oblige me and eat so that we can get on to more important things?"

Mrs. McGruder is a MORE person. Everything, no matter what it is, always should be MORE.

Together we went down the hall to the room that I was again to share with Rosemary and Mrs. McGruder looked at my bed and said that the sheets and spread could stand a little MORE smoothing and the pillow a little MORE plumping. Then she watched while I finished unpacking my suitcases which contained MORE books than clothes and said that I should have brought MORE dresses and that those I did bring needed MORE starch.

She looked at my white shoes and made a noise with her tongue against the roof of her mouth. "Who polished these shoes, Ellen Grae?"

"I did. Don't they look nice?"

"Yes. Except they've got MORE white on the soles than on the tops."

※※※

ABOUT TEN O'CLOCK we drove down to the village of Thicket to meet Rosemary's train but as usual it was late. Mrs. McGruder parked the car off to one side and tried to settle down to reading a magazine which she had had the foresight to bring along but couldn't because I was there.

"Goodness, Ellen Grae. Stop fidgeting."

"I'm not fidgeting. I'm itching myself. It's all those baths I've been taking. Wouldn't some boiled peanuts taste good right about now? Just to take our minds off things?"

Mrs. McGruder frowned but when she turned her head to look at me there was a gentleness in her eyes. "Oh, honey, you don't really want any boiled peanuts now, do you?"

"Some nice, salty, juicy ones. The way Ira fixes them. While we're just sitting here waiting for Rosemary I could just hop over to his stand and get us a couple of bags. I'd hurry."

Mrs. McGruder sighed but reached into her handbag and found her change purse and extracted a quarter. "All right but don't make me come after you. And watch when you cross the street."

She meant for cars, of course, but there were only three parked ones. First Street lay hot and quiet under the September sun. The only humans in sight were the clerk from Sangster's Grocery Store who was busy letting down the green window awnings, a man in white coveralls who had his head stuck in the door of the barber shop, and Ira who was setting up his stand in its customary oak-shaded spot.

A lot of people in Thicket think that Ira is crazy but he's not. He's just different. He never wears shoes even when the cold winds come sweeping down from the north, he can't read or write and he lives in a two-room tin shack down near the river bend all by himself. Mrs. McGruder told me that once upon a time Ira had a mother and father, at least a stepfather, but that one day they just picked up and left and never came back. Nobody knows how old Ira is. Mrs. McGruder says maybe thirty but I think maybe he's older because he's got white in his black hair and sometimes his dark eyes have a very old man's sadness in them. Ira lives on what money he can make selling boiled and parched peanuts and sometimes somebody patient will pay him to mow a yard. He could make a lot of money mowing yards because he's neat and careful but he won't talk to people. He just nods and points which makes everybody nervous. Even when he goes into a store to buy something that's all he does. Mrs. McGruder told me that in all the years she's been seeing Ira around town she's never heard him speak. I reckon nobody has except me. He talks to me all the time.

I skipped up to his stand and whacked the board that was his counter and said, "Hey, Ira."

He turned around and gave me his slow, quiet look. "Hey, Ellen Grae. I wuz hopin' you'd come by to see me this mornin'. I saw you yistiddy when you come on the train."

"You did? I didn't see you. Why didn't you holler?"

"They wuz people around. Ellen Grae, I got me a goat now."

"Oh, Ira, that's wonderful!"

"When can you come and see her?"

"I don't know. Maybe Sunday after church. I'll get Grover to come with me. I brought back a whole pile of books with me. If you want me to I'll bring one when I come and read you a story. What's your goat's name?"

"Missouri."

"Missouri? That's a funny name for a goat."

"My mother's name wuz Missouri," Ira explained softly, setting two waxed paper bags of boiled peanuts up on the counter. "My goat reminds me of my mother. Did I ever tell you what happened to my mother, Ellen Grae?"

I laid my quarter on the counter and waited for Ira to lay back a nickel change but he didn't. Which wasn't unusual. Ira didn't know how to make change. If you handed him a dollar for one bag of peanuts he'd keep the whole thing. But, by the same token, if you only handed him a penny for a half dozen bags that was all right too. So, if you traded with him for any length of time, things kind of evened themselves out.

"Yes, you told me what happened to your mother, Ira. Listen, I have to go now. Mrs. McGruder and I just came down to the train station to meet Rosemary. When Grover and I come over Sunday afternoon I'll read to you."

"She died in the swamp, she and her husband. While they wuz tryin' to run away from me. They had 'em this ol' rattler in a box and they wuz draggin' me alongside an' pokin' at him with a stick but instead of bitin' me like he wuz suppose' to, he stuck his ol' head out 'n bit 'em. They swoll up and threshed around some afterward but they wa'n't nothin' I could do for 'em. We wuz too far back in the swamp. So I buried 'em 'longside of that ol' snake. I killed the snake first so he wouldn't bite 'em no more. I didn't tell you 'bout this before, did I, Ellen Grae?"

"No, I reckon this is the first time, Ira. Listen, I'll see you Sunday." I picked up the two bags of peanuts and started to turn away and leave but something in the way Ira looked caused me to turn back. "Listen, Ira, you feel all right, don't you? You aren't sick or anything, are you?"

For a second I thought there were tears on Ira's black lashes but it was only the sun glinting on them. He said, "No, I'm not sick, Ellen Grae. Just tuckered out from talkin' so much."

Poor Ira. He has these hallucinations.

❊❊❊

ROSEMARY ARRIVED, her same old gloomy self. As soon as we got back to the McGruders' she started in with her griping. "Well, I can see that nothing much has changed," she commented, flouncing herself around our bedroom with such vigor that the lace of her pink pants showed. "Even that crack on the ceiling's the same. I wish somebody'd tell me why I can't stay home and go to school and be comfortable instead of having to come down here and do it. How much gum have you got in your mouth, Ellen Grae?"

"Four sticks. You want a piece?"

"Oh, God," Rosemary said with a lot of fervor.

I perched myself on the footrail of my bed. "Don't swear, Rosemary. The reason you're here is the same reason I'm here. Our parents are divorced and our fathers have to put us in the charge of somebody they can trust. And they trust Mrs. McGruder because she went to the same high school your father and my father did, and she's a nice, homey woman who'll teach us manners and see to it that we get educated and won't corrupt our morals."

"Oh, Ellen Grae, I know all that. Will you please stop smacking that gum? Spit it out. You're making me nervous."

"Everything makes you nervous. Is that a new ring you have on, Rosemary?"

"Yes. My father bought it for me as a going-away present. He's going to send me a watch for my birthday."

"My, you're lucky. I wish I had a rich father. But

I reckon to be rich you've got to want to be and Jeff doesn't. I reckon he'll die penniless in a garret."

"A what?"

"A garret. One of those places where people put all their old magazines and other stuff they're tired of. People die in them. *All* artists die in garrets."

"I *wish* Mr. McGruder would fix that crack in the ceiling," Rosemary said irritably. "He *is* still here, isn't he? Have you seen him?"

"I saw him yesterday right after I got here. He was roller-skating out on the sidewalk in front of the house."

Rosemary turned and stared at me. "I'm talking about Mr. McGruder. Are you?"

"Of course. That's who you asked me about, isn't it? He was roller-skating on one skate which that dumb kid next door had left out on the sidewalk. Today he's in bed. The doctor said he might have to be put in traction."

"In what?"

"Traction. You know. Where they hoist one leg up and attach it to the ceiling? Jeff had to be put in traction once. He couldn't even scratch himself. Grace and I had to do it for him. That's before she and Jeff got a divorce."

"How disgusting. My father wouldn't ask me to scratch him even if he was dying. My father would never dream of letting me see him with one leg fastened to the ceiling. You've got a peculiar family, Ellen Grae."

"I know it. For centuries all of us Derryberrys have been peculiar. We can't help ourselves."

"I told my father that you called your parents by their first names and he couldn't believe it. Please brush your hair out of your eyes, Ellen Grae. The way it hangs down like that makes me nervous. Why do you let it do it?"

"I don't. It just does. You should see Grace's. It's worse than mine. If Jeff ever sells a painting maybe I'll ask for the money to have some big fat curls put in. Like yours. But for right now I guess I'll just have to slop along like I am. Mrs. McGruder dyed the curtains in here. Did you notice?"

"Hideous. They remind me of measles. At home we have everything white. Even the rugs and chairs."

"I saw a white chair once. In a doctor's office. I almost wept it was so beautiful. The doctor said he'd never seen anybody get so emotional over a piece of furniture. They had to pry me away from it."

Rosemary's smile was pale. "Oh, honestly, Ellen Grae."

"It's the truth. It took the nurse and Jeff and the doctor, all three of them, to pry me away from it. The doctor said if I was younger he might be able to understand it but as it was, my case had him baffled. He wanted to call in a psychiatrist but Jeff didn't have any money. All he had was a picture of a light pole he'd painted and the doctor didn't want that so we had to leave. When we got home Jeff got out a can of paint and took one of our old brown chairs and painted it nice, shiny white and for a while I was comforted. Poor Jeff. I'm afraid he'll never amount to much of anything. He just doesn't have enough education. The Sorbonne didn't teach him how to do anything except paint and speak foreign languages. Does your father ever speak to you in a foreign language, Rosemary?"

"Of course not. He's an American."

"Yes, I know that but I just thought that he might have picked up a few foreign words somewhere. Of course in his business I guess it wouldn't do him any good even if he had. People who borrow money want you to lend it to them in American, don't they? I told Jeff about your father being manager for a finance company but I wish I hadn't. It just made him feel inferior. Listen, Rosemary, aren't you going to unpack? There are plenty of hangers. I only used six. Want me to help you?"

Rosemary's thick, white face filled with impatient contempt. "Thanks but no thanks. Your hands are never clean enough to suit me. At home when Helen—she's our maid—hangs up my clothes I always make her wash her hands first. I wish I could have this room to myself. I'll be thirteen my next birthday and I think it's a positive disgrace that I have to room with a little eleven-year-old kid."

"I think it's a disgrace too, Rosemary. I know it's harder on you than it is on me but I guess we'll just have to make the best of it. Actually, except for the way you twitch and mutter in your sleep and the way you move your lips when you read I really don't mind sharing this room with you, Rosemary."

"I don't move my lips when I read."

"Yes, you do. But maybe I have some bad habits that you don't like too. I tell you what. I'll list all the things you do that I don't like on a piece of paper and you list all the things I do that you don't like on a piece of paper, and we'll exchange papers and each of us will take steps, and maybe we'll get along better than we did last year. Okay?"

Rosemary showed me the whites of her eyes but she said, "Okay. I think we'd better wait until after lunch to do it though because my list isn't going to be just three things like muttering and twitching and moving lips. I've got a long string of things I don't like about you. It'll take me at least thirty minutes to put them all down."

That was an exaggeration but her list, when she finally completed it and with her eyebrows raised to haughty peaks, handed it to me, *was* startling. It complained that my books were everywhere, even under the bed, and that I kept her awake chortling over them or grumbling or making squeaks hopping in and out of bed to run over and consult the dictionary.

It deplored the fact that I didn't share her passion for soap and water, a tidy dresser top, brushed hair with ribbons in it to keep it from flopping, petticoats so that nobody'd ever suspect that I had pants and legs underneath, Sunday school, her father's photograph, clean, polite boys, conversation, dress-up parties, and love movies. It bemoaned the fact that I didn't look like a girl, that I was always eating cheese which made my breath stink, that I used words even when they didn't fit just to impress people and that my choice of friends embarrassed her.

"Which of my friends embarrass you?" I asked.

She gave me a slippery, sidelong look that was supposed to convey something but didn't.

"That crazy Ira, for one."

"Ira's not crazy."

"If he isn't why doesn't he talk to people?"

"He does. He talks to me."

"Ha! I'll bet he's never said one word to you that made any sense. Even his parents couldn't stand him because he's so crazy. They ran away and left him. Everybody in this town knows that."

"Which of my other friends embarrass you, Rosemary?"

"That dumb old Grover."

"Grover's not dumb."

"Sure he is; he should be a grade ahead of you but he isn't. He's twelve and still only in the sixth grade, same as you. Why is that?"

"Because when his mother killed herself he stayed out of school for a year. You shouldn't say mean things about Grover, Rosemary. He says nice things about you."

"What does he say about me?" Rosemary demanded with dark suspicion.

I tried to think fast but the only thing that I could make pop into my mind was a textbook phrase that Jeff had laboriously taught me. *He is glad that you have so much money.* "Il est heureux que vous ayez tant d'argent," I said in French and threw myself backward on the bed, making myself shake with forced laughter.

Rosemary's face puckered and I think she would have started to bawl if Mrs. McGruder hadn't come

in just then and said how would we like to take a
ride with her out to the chicken ranch and get eggs?

XXX

ROSEMARY IS a matutinophobe and I'm a matutino-
phile. I jump out of bed with a song in my heart every morning. Even if it's raining I'm glad. But this
morning it wasn't. The dawn was cool with a color-
less sky and a silver mist hanging between the trees.
There was the feel of Saturday and the smell of a
completed summer in the air. Beyond the McGruders'
gate the road stretched out like a ribbon, dry and
brown. At the end of the road is the gaunt house
where Grover lives.

He never acts surprised to see me. With two cold
biscuit and ham sandwiches in his hand he came to the
screen door and blinked his brown eyes a couple of
times and then came out on the porch and handed me
one of the sandwiches and said, "Hey, Ellen Grae.
You back?"

"No, this is my ghost come to visit you."

He searched the inside of one ear with a brown
finger. "Why you pantin'?"

"I'm not panting. I'm just breathing. Walking down
here I breathed three hundred and fourteen times. I
controlled it though so it didn't hurt me. I know a
girl who didn't control her breathing and breathed so
hard the wrong way that her eyeballs fell out."

"I didn't know there was a wrong way and a right
way to breathe."

"Sure there is. Singers and people who make
speeches all the time go to school to learn to breathe
right."

Grover placed one hand on his bare stomach and
breathed. "I think I'd rather be deaf than blind."

"Who's blind?"

"The girl whose eyeballs fell out. Didn't you say
her eyeballs fell out?"

"Yes, but she's not blind."

"She isn't?"

"No. She would have been but fortunately her father's a famous eye surgeon and he quick got two eyeballs from somebody else in the hospital where he works who'd just died and put them in this girl's sockets and she can see just as good as ever. The only thing is in his frantic haste he overlooked the fact that one of the eyeballs was green and the other black. She's in the movies now and her father isn't a doctor any more. They live in Hollywood, California now. Listen, Grover, this ham is so salty I'm about to gag. Could I have a drink of water?"

"It's well water," Grover warned. "Last year you said *that* made you gag."

"I know I did but that was last year. I've changed my mind about a lot of things since then. One of them's water. Did you know that country people live longer than city people just because they drink pure water?"

"No, I didn't know that."

"Well, they do. You ever see a country person with calcified bones?"

"No, I don't think so."

"Of course not. But all city people have them—even me. What causes them is all the stuff they put in the water tanks to purify it. A man fell in our city water tank last Christmas Eve day while he was up there painting a sign that said Joy To The World on the side of it, and they didn't find his body until it had all come apart and now practically everybody in the city is calcified."

In three bites Grover consumed his sandwich, left the porch, and walked across the yard to the spring-fed well and pumped and came back with a tin dipper of water and handed it to me. While I drank he scratched himself.

"I fixed the boat so it doesn't leak any more and I got me a flag and some oars for it now. You want to go fishing?"

"I reckon I do. I left a note for Mrs. McGruder. She'll jaw at me when I get back but by that time it'll be too late. Let's go."

"Wait," Grover said and went back into the house and was gone a couple of minutes. When he came back out he had his shirt and shoes on, and carried a whole roasted chicken and two bananas in a plastic bag. "It's all I could find," he apologized. "But it'll taste good about noon. Let's go."

The parched fields between Grover's house and the river lay passive, brittle underfoot, and filled with the dusty scent of dried roots and dehydrated underbrush. The sun climbed steadily, clean and hot. A cloud of black gnats found us and Grover grabbed my hand and we ran, panting and sweating and stirring up little puffs of choking dirt with our feet, until we reached the river bank. Sweet, cool air rushed up and out to meet us. The boat, tied to a water oak, bobbed with the motion of the water. Grover had painted the outside of it gray and the inside a glistening red. The flag, attached to the stern, made it look official. Two cane poles, a bait bucket, and a small shovel rested beneath a piece of canvas in its bottom.

Grover took off his shoes and slid down and climbed into the boat and stored the chicken and bananas and returned with the bucket and shovel. We dug pink worms from his worm bed and deposited them in the bucket along with plenty of damp, black earth. I lost a few of them getting in the boat—the bucket clanged against the side—and Grover gave me a look and muttered something about girls being clumsy but we didn't have words like we sometimes did when he said that because I swallowed my temper.

The river, broad and tranquil and gently curving, welcomed us like an old friend. We paddled out into the middle of it and Grover, trying to look and act nautical, stood up in the bow, shaded his eyes with his hand even though there wasn't much sun because of the overhanging trees, scanned the water and both banks, and said, "Rest your oar, Ellen Grae."

I rested my oar.

"I'm going to catch a fish," Grover said. "Hand me a worm."

I handed him a worm.

"Aren't you going to fish?" he inquired, wrestling around with one of the cane poles and a hook and the worm.

"Not for the nonce. For the nonce I just want to sit here and let nature exert her wonderful powers of healing o'er my bruised spirit."

Grover lowered his pole into the water and sat down, placing his back against one side of the boat's hull and planting his feet against the other, preparing for a heavy strike. "What's it bruised from?"

"My spirit? My spirit's not bruised, Grover. How could it be? I was just trying that out on you to see what you'd say. What'd it make you think of when I said it?"

"A lady who's dying," Grover said unexpectedly. "What's it make you think of?"

"A monk with a hood over his face weeping for humanity."

"Do monks weep for humanity?"

"Some of them do. I knew a monk once who spent his whole life doing nothing but weeping for humanity. All he did was sit around in doorways and beg alms to keep his poor wracked body together and weep for humanity. The sounds that came out of him were terrible. I'll never forget them. The day before he died he gave me his Bible. I'll show it to you sometime. He was from Scotland and in the Book of Psalms he left a piece of pressed heather. I guess the poor thing yearned for his country, even to the last. I had to sneak the Bible out of the sanitarium; he was tubercular."

Grover wrapped a denim leg around the pole and with a dirt-crusted toe jiggled it. He turned a solemn, brown gaze on me. "I've never seen a monk but

I knew a lady who came from Scotland once. She was born with her head in her arm pit. She told me that lots of people over there are born that way. It's some kind of a curse or something. She was sure ugly. Nobody but me could stand to look at her. Not even her husband. He used to pay me fifty cents a week to take food to her. She died from eating too much peanut butter; when they embalmed her they had to stop when they got to her stomach because it was glued together with peanut butter. At her funeral her husband fainted and fell in the grave with her and all of her relatives who'd come over from Scotland to pay their last respects fell to their knees in the mud. They all looked like this lady I'm telling you about and had to spend the night at the funeral home because the hotel wouldn't rent them a room. The funeral director said they cried all night long but said it wasn't like any crying he'd ever heard before. They were polite though and didn't make any mess and paid him and every once in a while now he gets a box from them with sweaters in them. The only thing is the neck holes are always in the wrong place. I guess they keep forgetting that everybody's not born with their head in their arm pit."

I studied the cypress trees on the river banks. Festooned with Spanish moss they looked like old, gray-bearded men. Two birds sailing wing-to-wing overhead dipped low and one of them made droppings on the bow of the boat. With a look of bland contentment Grover sucked his cheeks.

"That's the most utter story I ever heard," I said after some thought.

"Whad'ya mean, utter?"

"I mean utter. Put anything after it you want but it's utter."

"Then there was this other man I knew from Scotland who ate oat cakes all the time. Nothing but oat cakes. And roamed the moors at night, mourning."

"For his departed ancestors, I suppose."

"Yes. For his departed ancestors. One night he asked me to go along. It was raining sheets and black as soot and every once in awhile there'd be this great big bolt of lightning——"

"——that tore up trees and hurled bodies through the air but you and your friend stepped out in your long black capes——"

"——and roamed the moor all night. Afterward I had pneumonia and had to stay in bed for three days and in my delirium I told my father where I'd been to get sick and at first he didn't believe me. He said there wasn't anybody around here like that . . . that I'd dreamed it all——"

"——but one night there was a tapping at the window and your father went to see what it was and there stood your friend from Scotland in his black cape."

"Yes," Grover said, grinning.

"Grover, those are the two worst stories I ever heard in my whole life. You certainly don't expect me to believe them, do you?"

"Why not? They're as true as most of the ones you tell me."

"I beg your pardon?"

"I wish a two-pound catfish would come along and grab hold of this hook," he said. "I just wrote a poem. You want to hear it?"

"A poem? I didn't know you could write poetry."

"I didn't either until just a minute ago. But here's what I wrote:

IN A DOORWAY SAT A HUNK OF A MONK.
HE WAS PRAYING AND BEGGING AND STUNK.
HE STANK BECAUSE HE DRUNK.
HE DRANK BECAUSE OF ELLEN GRAE'S BUNK!

Without appetite the river's smooth tongue pushed and licked at the stern and sides of the boat. Off our bow a fish jumped but Grover ignored it. "Did you like my poem?" he asked with a clear, innocent expression and both of us burst out laughing.

It was good out there on the river with the sunlight dappling the brown water and the soft, intermingling odors of the forest all around. We saw two otters sunning themselves on the river bank and a blue heron standing stiff-legged on a cypress knee. Grover stood up and hooted at it but it didn't move. Far off to our right a giant bullfrog thumped out a throaty basso lament and was answered by a timid, soprano peep. We reached the bend in the river and I sat up straight and looked hard toward Ira's shack and saw Missouri tugging on a towel or something that was hanging from the clothesline, but Ira wasn't anywhere about.

"I been readin' about buried treasure," Grover said, plying his oar with red-faced energy. "I'll bet there's lots of it around here just waitin' for somebody to come along and dig it up. Let's you and me bring a coupla shovels out here next Saturday and root around. Want to?"

"Sure. We'll bring Ira along. He can be our guide. He knows this swamp better than anybody. You got him to talk to you yet?"

"Some. I took him and his goat fishin' about a month ago. He talked to me some then."

"What'd he talk about?"

"Nothin'. His goat's name is Missouri. He said he named it after his mother."

On Sunday Grover and I didn't get to go to Ira's place so that I could read to him because it rained. We didn't go to Sunday school or church either because Mrs. McGruder was coming down with a cold and Mr. McGruder was still limping from his roller-skating accident.

For dinner we had roast leg of lamb with mint jelly.

Rosemary griped.

In the afternoon everybody except me took a nap. I read a book and watched Rosemary, who sleeps with her eyes partly open which can be a little frightening in the dead of night but which in the day-time is interesting. The lower ovals of them, with stiff fans of brown hair above and beneath them, gleam whitely and with every breath roll and turn in their watery sockets. Her mouth, painted a cold, gleaming purple with lipstick, which she isn't allowed to wear in Mrs. McGruder's presence, pulls back from her teeth in secret mirth.

About two o'clock I finished my book and the rain stopped and I went up to the attic and opened a window and leaned out and watched a rainbow appear. The glow from it touched the meadows, lacquering them with gold and the foot of it dipped deep into the swamp beyond.

✕✕✕

CAME LABOR DAY which Mrs. McGruder believes in. She and Mr. McGruder washed every window and hosed down the outside of the house.

Rosemary and I polished all of our shoes and examined all of our dresses and slips and pants for missing buttons and open seams and tears. We straightened our room and washed our hair. To make it shine I put vinegar on mine and Rosemary put a cream rinse on hers.

"Grover and I are going treasure hunting next Saturday," I told her. "You wouldn't want to come along, would you?"

"No thank you."

"You'd have a good time. It's lots of fun rowing up and down the river."

She anchored a fat curl to one temple with four hairpins. A thin spark of interest came into her face. "Well, I *might* be interested when the time comes. I wouldn't have to help row, would I?"

"No. Ira's going to come with us. He and Grover will do the rowing."

The interest died. She said, "Oh. Oh, I don't think I want to go, Ellen Grae. You wouldn't want to come home when I'd want to and the sun's bad for my skin. But thank you for asking me. Thank you a lot."

Came Tuesday and we went off to school. I took my petticoat off when I got there and stuck it in my desk. Mrs. McGruder believes in lots of starch and I don't; I like my clothes limply comfortable.

Right away we got down to the business of getting educated. For our first homework assignment Miss Daniels, the new English teacher, said for us to write a short story and use the words allege and accusation and akimbo in it. So that night I wrote a story about Albert, a seamy man from the Allegheny Mountains who was alleged to be mean and brutal but who was really, in truth, very lovely and gentle. One day when he realized the true meaning of all the accusations the town people had been making against him he climbed up to the top of a blue hill and stood there, his arms akimbo, and swore his revenge.

Miss Daniels said that my story met all of the requirements and she kept me after school so that we could talk about it.

"Of what was Albert being accused?" she inquired. "That point wasn't quite clear to me."

"It wasn't quite clear to me either," I confessed. "I just knew there had to be some accusations for something so I stuck it in there."

"What makes you think a hill is blue?" she asked. "Have you ever seen a blue hill?"

"Yes, ma'am. I've seen hills all colors. Green, black, brown, purple. But I believe the blue ones are the prettiest."

She said, "Your handwriting is really quite terrible. I think we must work on that."

"Yes, ma'am."

"You must learn to keep your margins neat and write straight across and form each letter. Letters are not supposed to lean on one another. Each is supposed to stand on its own."

"Yes, ma'am."

She touched the white froth that was her collar. "But I liked your blue hill," she said.

Before Grace and Jeff got their divorce we always went to a Chinese restaurant on Thursday nights and then went home to do the wash and hang it on pulley lines. If there was a night breeze it would flap and keep us awake. We were up so high with just building tops all around and the washes of other moneyless people hanging like tired skeletons on other swinging lines. But Thursday night at the McGruders' usually brought Pigs in the Blanket, which was hamburger baked in biscuit dough, or Pigs in the Sheet, which was hamburger boiled in cabbage leaves, and then afterward Rosemary and I studied. We were not allowed to watch television.

Friday was general assembly day at school. Sometimes, after all the announcements and stuff, somebody with talent would get up on the stage and perform. There was this boy who had a sousaphone and knew how to play it but somebody poured water in it and when he came strutting out and started to play for us no music came out—just gurgles. Everybody laughed.

❧❧❧

SATURDAY, STILL AND YELLOW and hot, arrived. The minute I went to the window and looked out at it I knew that it was going to be different. A hummingbird with a ruby throat and an emerald head hovered motionless above a pale hibiscus blossom, his wing tips whistling. As I watched he delicately settled himself on the flower, stuck his bill into it and drank. Beneath the hibiscus bush the grass with droplets of night moisture on it sparkled green.

Rosemary's eyes were completely closed and her mouth, without lipstick, looked clean and kind.

In the kitchen Mr. McGruder, who was the only

one up besides me, set two buckwheat pancakes in front of me and without thinking I ate them both. He wanted to know why I was up so early.

"It's not early," I said. "It's six o'clock. Grover and I are going treasure hunting."

Mr. McGruder looked vague and hid himself behind the morning paper.

"Ira is going with us," I said. "We'll be gone most all day. Will you tell Mrs. McGruder so she won't worry?"

Deep in his paper Mr. McGruder said, "Sure."

"Is it okay if I fix some sandwiches and stuff for our lunch?"

"Sure. Go ahead."

"And can I borrow your square shovel?"

"Help yourself."

Mr. McGruder is a very generous man.

Between the McGruders' house and Grover's there lay a shimmering calm. The sky, streaked with pennants of bright rose, was motionless. A cardinal swung from a streamer of Spanish moss. There was the smell of mimosa and dog fennel and flowering honeysuckle in the air.

Outside of Grover's house I hollered for him and he came trotting. "Hey, Ellen Grae. You bring everything I told you to? You didn't forget to bring Mr. McGruder's shovel, did you?"

"Oh, Grover, I sure did. This thing you see here in my hand is a wand."

Until we paddled down the river and collected Ira and Missouri there wasn't anybody for Grover to take charge of except me, but he pulled his shoulders back and squared his face and clipped out commands. I was ordered to carry the shovel, my sack of lunch, a coil of rope, a bottle of insect repellent, a small first-aid kit, and a jar of foul-smelling salve which had healing powers. Grover carried another sack of lunch, another shovel, and a hatchet to hack our way through the forest. I was ordered not to talk—to save my energy for the walk to the river and the boat. So in silence we set out.

The shovel was heavy and I had to keep shifting it from one hand to the other. The muscles in my upper arms quivered from the strain. A covey of fat-chested quail flashed across our path. Strong and gathering heat, the sun climbed. A bug stung me on my cheek and when we got to the boat Grover put ammonia on it. "If you'd watch where you're going you wouldn't get stung," he said. "Does it hurt?"

"Oh no. It feels good. I like being stung by bugs."

He put the cap back on the ammonia bottle. "Don't talk. Save your energy for rowing."

We rowed down the river and when we got to the bend altered our course and put in and picked up Ira and Missouri. Missouri came into the boat without being coaxed and when Ira climbed in and sat down in the bow, went to him and laid her head in his lap. Ira took a lump of sugar from his shirt pocket and offered it to her and she looked at him and flicked her red tongue out and gathered it into her mouth and swallowed it whole.

"I washed her yistiddy," Ira said, his black eyes full of light. "Say somethin' to her, Ellen Grae."

I said, "Hey, Missouri." And she left Ira and came to me, pushing her wiry body against my knees.

"Let's shove off," Grover said, his mouth square and hard. And Ira, without being told, moved to the stern and took up an oar and dipped it into the water and with beautiful ease we moved out of the cove and back into the river. Like a dog, Missouri lifted her head and pointed her nose into the wind. I put my hand on her clean, white back and she grunted trustingly. Her horns, curving gently backward, gleamed like polished glass.

Grover, in the bow of the boat, said, "How far down river you reckon we ought to go, Ira?"

"A piece," Ira answered.

So, gliding through the brown water, we went on down river a piece to where it narrowed and the sunlight struggled to get through the dark, over-hanging trees and the swamp rose up on both sides of us, dank and cool and spiked with clumps of coarse grass and wild fern and stumps. The land looked solid but Ira, with a look of unease, said, "Ellen Grae?"

"What, Ira?"

"We best go back a piece."

"Why? What's wrong with it here?"

Ira turned his head and looked at Missouri. "We best go back a piece."

Grover laid his oar aside, hung his head over the side of the boat and splashed water into his face. "We'll go back pretty soon, Ira. As soon as we eat and have a look around. Break out the lunch, Ellen Grae."

I broke out the lunch and divided it four ways. Missouri refused a drumstick but crunched happily on an apple.

"Where you reckon all this treasure we're supposed to look for is?" I asked Grover. "If you ask me I don't think any of it's back here. This is just swamp."

"Sure it's swamp. That's what we want. Swamp. In the olden days, before the government made them go live on reservations, Indians used to live back here. I got a book from the library and read up on it and found out."

"Found out what?"

"That they didn't have any money then. They used fishhooks made out of gold for money."

"And you figure they left some of these hooks behind?"

Grover's brown eyes spurned my realism. "I figure they might have. But we aren't out here just to look for gold fishhooks. We'll take anything we can find. The Spaniards used to own this land before America did and they were rich. But they were always fightin' with the Americans and the Indians. If some of them had to run off in a hurry you think they'd stop to drag all their stuff along?"

"Gee, Grover, I don't know. I never thought about it."

Grover put a finger between two shirt buttons and reached inside and scratched. A strange kind of soft, sweet excitement crept into his eyes. "We aren't too far from the ocean. A lot of Spanish ships used to be wrecked off of this coast and the sailors used to come in here and hide while they were waitin' for other ships to come by and pick them up. They buried stuff from their ships when they couldn't take it along. Silverware and money and jewelry. We'd be rich if we could find just one piece, Ellen Grae."

"How do we know where to dig?"

"You look for mounds and sunken places. Some treasure hunters use mine detectors but they cost about twenty dollars even in army surplus stores."

Ira said, "We best go back a piece, Ellen Grae."

"We'll go pretty soon, Ira. But first we want to look around a little. You know this part of the swamp, don't you? You've been here before, haven't you?"

Ira's half smile was shy and slow and uncertain. "I bin here before I think."

"Sure you have," Grover said, hearty and vigorous and eager. "So you take Missouri and go first and Ellen Grae and me'll follow. Look for us a good place to dig. Watch out for mounds and sunken places, Ira."

Missouri, anticipating, went to stand in the bow of the boat and Ira went up and climbed off, and then lifted her to the bank. They stood there for a second and then Missouri lifted her head and sniffed and made a noise and Ira, with his hand, gave her his consent to go. She made another noise and broke away from him and wheeled and streaked off through the dense swamp growth, her dainty legs flashing. Ira followed her. In just a minute or two they were lost from our sight.

The forest sighed and rustled and murmured.

Grover said, "He didn't want to stay here for some reason. But I think our chances are as good here as they are anywhere else; maybe better. At least it's not as marshy here as it is on back a ways. Ira'll find us a good likely lookin' spot. He knows what we're after. He's not as dumb as some people think he is. Break out your shovel, Ellen Grae."

I broke out my shovel.

"You're not like most girls," Grover said. "I don't have to tell you that if you're going to look for buried treasure you got to get out of the boat."

I laid the shovel across my shoulder and by myself struggled out of the bobbing boat. Grover, with the other shovel and the hatchet, followed.

"Watch where you're goin'," Grover ordered.

"Which way did Ira go?"

"This way. Lordy, it's hot."

"It's gonna get hotter. We oughta get somethin' done before the heat tuckers us out."

All around us the swamp lay deep in its ancient silence. Making our own path as we went, we came upon a stand of grass containing a ground nest full of eggs so glossy they looked like porcelain and very deep in color. Grover knelt and examined them. "Probably ducks," he said. "Ira might know. Where the heck is he?"

I peered through the trees ahead but didn't see Ira. I hollered for him but just the echo of my own voice, high and eerie, answered.

"These eggs are the prettiest I've ever seen," Grover said, engrossed in them. "They look like they've been dyed. I'd sure like to know what kind they are. Go on up ahead a little, Ellen Grae. Ira's up there doin' somethin'. Tell him I want him to come back here and look at these eggs."

I laid my shovel down and tightened the belt to my pants. "There might be quicksand around here."

"Ain't no quicksand around here. Go on."

Ten minutes later I found Ira standing beside a sunken place in the earth's floor. Missouri, her tail a stiff white plume, stood motionless beside him. The sun had penetrated the treetops and lay in a bright pool on the sunken place, the man, and the goat.

Ira had his back to me and didn't turn until I went up to him and laid my hand on his arm.

I said, "Hey, Ira, what's the matter? Why are you just standing here? Grover's found a nest full of eggs and wants you to come back and look at them. Come on."

He looked down at me and I saw then the pain and sorrow in him. There were tears in his eyes. He said, "Ellen Grae, you remember I told you what happened to my mother and her husband?"

"Yes, Ira, I remember but——"

"They had 'em this snake in a box and they wuz draggin' me alongside and pokin' at him with a stick . . ."

"Ira, I remember! I told you I remember! I don't want to hear about it anymore now! Come on, let's go back to where Grover is."

". . . but instead of bitin' me like he wuz suppose' to he stuck his head out and bit them."

I looked at the sunken place and my stomach shifted.

Missouri made a sound in her throat.

"I didn't know what to do, Ellen Grae. We didn't come here in any boat. I didn't know what to do so I . . ."

"Ira, I told you I didn't want to hear about it anymore! You've told me about it a thousand times and I'm sick of it! Come on! Grover's waiting for us. He wants you to look at some duck eggs."

". . . I buried 'em," he whispered and stepped back away from me and out of the pool of sunlight.

My voice didn't belong to me. It had a bottomless calm. It said, "All right, Ira, let's go back now. Grover's found a nest full of eggs and wants you to look at them."

He let me take him by the hand then and we walked away from the place. Missouri trotted beside us. She didn't look back and neither did Ira nor I.

Ira couldn't identify the eggs. He said he had seen

lots of them in the swamp but didn't know what kind they were.

I said that I had a headache, one of the worst I'd ever had in my whole life, and wanted to go home.

Grover wasn't very sympathetic. He said it looked to him like I could have got my headache over with the day before if I had to have one. He wanted to know why we had to be in such an all-fired hurry. He got very mad at me.

✕✕✕

IN THE SWAMP, beneath a blanket of dirt, with nothing between them and it, lay Ira's mother and her husband put there by Ira, and I alone knew this dark and heavy secret. How was I going to manage to keep this to myself? Little secrets weren't hard to keep but this one wasn't little. It was threatening. If I didn't keep it what would happen to my friend Ira who had never on purpose harmed a soul in his whole life? Would he be sent to the crazy house or to jail?

Were their faces raised in their death sleep to the rain and the sun? How far beneath the earth's surface were they buried? Far enough so that the wind wouldn't blow away their blanket and expose them? Oh, surely Ira would have had enough sense to bury them deeply—he had a lot of primitive intelligence.

But it wasn't right. Dead people, even bad ones, belonged in cemeteries with markers at their heads to let people know when they had been born and when they had died. Maybe there was somebody besides Ira who had cared about them and, if they knew, would want to come and stand beside their cradle and cry and put flowers. But no one would ever know about these two except Ira and me. They would lie there in the swamp, still and cold, forever with the snake coiled beside them, the last of his evils done.

I did my best not to think about it. I crammed my mind with all kinds of things—stuff I didn't even care about, hoping that if I filled it full enough and kept it busy enough it would forget. But slyly the secret clung.

It brought a change in me. Came a hunger for food which had only been of small interest before.

"You act like you've got a tapeworm," Rosemary said. "The way you stuff yourself. All that food you eat you ought to weigh a ton but, my, you're skinny. I wouldn't be as skinny as you for anything."

And came this thirst for sleep. "You used to get up with the roosters," Mrs. McGruder commented. "Now I can't force you out of bed. Are you sure you're not sick?"

"No, ma'am, I'm not sick. I'm just tired."

Mr. McGruder, who was a male nurse in his youth, said that my lethargy could be diabetes or some other serious disease.

I was hustled off to the doctor. His hair grew in red powder puffs on each side of his head but none on top and his palms, soft and dry, whispered when he rubbed them together. The toes of his shoes were a dark, brilliant ebony.

We sat down in his white office and he said, "All right now, Ellen Grae."

"Sir?"

"Do you hurt anywhere?"

"No, sir."

"Not one little pain or ache anywhere?"

"No, sir."

"Mrs. McGruder tells me that all you want to do lately is sleep. Is that true?"

"I reckon it is."

"Why is this do you suppose?"

"I don't know. Maybe it's because I don't have anything to stay awake for."

This doctor had very white, very beautiful teeth. When he smiled I could see that two of his back ones were hooked on to two of his side ones with tiny, silver prongs. He said, "Do you go to the bathroom a lot?"

"Sometimes. If I drink a lot of water I do."

"And do you drink a lot of water?"

"Sometimes."

"Are you thirsty now?"

"No, sir."

"Are you sleepy now?"

"No, sir."

The doctor showed me his silver prongs again. He said, "Well, I think we'd better have a look at you."

Naturally he didn't find anything because there wasn't anything. My tonsils were the right size, I didn't have rales in my chest, my kneecaps and elbows jumped when hit with his little hammer signifying that I had the proper reflexes. I had the right number of red corpuscles and white corpuscles in my blood and I didn't have any sugar in my urine. He couldn't look inside my skull and see the trouble that was hidden deep there, visible to no man, a tricky, brooding piece of knowledge, swarthy and insidious. He wrote out two prescriptions and I went with Mrs. McGruder to the drugstore and waited in a booth with her while the druggist filled them.

She ordered two cherry smashes and while we were drinking them she said, "Well, I'm glad there's nothing physically wrong with you."

"Yes, ma'am, I'm glad there's nothing physically wrong with me too."

"But I think if I had my choice I'd rather be physically disturbed than mentally. What about you?"

"I think that'd be better. Yes, ma'am."

"Your manners are improving," she said. "I'm glad to see that."

"Thank you, ma'am."

"But I don't know. I kind of liked you the other way too. I haven't had a good story out of you lately," she said.

"No, ma'am. I don't know any."

"You remember the one you told me about Fortis Alonzo Gridley?"

"Yes, ma'am, I remember."

Her green eyes had corners of shadow in them. "I told it to the girls at my bridge club and all of them thought it was very funny."

"It wasn't a true story, Mrs. McGruder. All of it was a lie. I made it up."

The shadows in her eyes came out of the corners and darkened all of the white and green in them and her voice softened the way it did when anybody in her house was sick and needed attention. She said, "No, it wasn't a lie. It was a story. You tell wonderful stories, Ellen Grae."

"I don't think I do but thank you."

Mrs. McGruder turned her head and her eyes traveled across the black and white checkerboard floor to a counter where a girl in a blue smock with a numbered button on its front was prettily arranging a pyramid of pink boxes. She said, "Honey, I wish you'd tell me what it is that's troubling you."

"Nothing's troubling me, Mrs. McGruder. The cherry smash was good. I thank you for it."

"Rosemary said she heard you crying in your sleep last night."

"Well, I don't know why she said that. You know I never cry even when I'm awake. Tears are useless; I found that out a long time ago. Jeff taught me. None of us Derryberrys cry about things."

Mrs. McGruder sighed but didn't say anything more. The druggist came with the prescriptions which were just vitamins and we went home and Mrs. McGruder baked macaroni and cheese and apple dumplings for supper and I ate so much that I couldn't concentrate on my homework afterward and later on, just before I went to bed, it all came up.

I had this dream about Ira. In it he was sitting on a stool in a room far away from the river and Missouri and there was sun which lay in bars across his shoulders and face. His beautiful hair had turned solid white and looked coarse and his feet, without any socks on them, had been stuffed into hard, pointed shoes. In this dream I saw myself go up some steps which were gray and cold and at the top was a door with a window in it. I went over to it and rapped on the glass and Ira rose and shuffled over and slid the pane back and peered out at me.

I said, "Hey, Ira. It's me. Ellen Grae."

His black eyes, very dry and very old, regarded me. "You went and told on me," he said. "I didn't think you'd do that, Ellen Grae."

"Oh, Ira, I didn't want to! I'm your friend! Really I am!"

"I thought you wuz," he said. "I thought you wuz my friend but you went and told on me."

"Ira, I had to! You have *got* to understand that! I didn't know they'd put you in here, honest I didn't! You're my friend! I wouldn't ever do anything to hurt you on purpose!"

With a terrible sadness and longing in his face he said, "You wuz my friend. The onliest one I ever had. And you went and told on me. Good-bye, Ellen Grae. Good-bye. Good-bye. Good-bye."

The last thing I remember seeing in the dream was his feet as he turned and limped back to his stool. Above the stiff leather that bound them I saw the ankles puffed, with the bones straining, and I felt the pain in them and in the darkness surrounding my bed there came this sound, clenched and low, which woke me and I realized that I was the one making it. I didn't go back to sleep for fear of other sounds I might make and other dreams I might dream.

At school I saw Grover every day. He said that he had had a chance to do some more reading about buried treasure and where in the United States it might be found and that his first calculations had been wrong. That it wasn't in any swamp or near any swamp.

His interest in it had cooled, he told me one afternoon while we were walking home. "I've got a job now," he said. "I'm learning how to be a veterinarian. My uncle is teaching me and he pays me three dollars every time I work all day. A dollar and a half if I only work till noon. Ellen Grae, are you listening to me?"

"Yes, Grover, I'm listening."

"That's where I was last Saturday. That's why I didn't come and ask you to go fishing or do something else. I had to go out to the country and help my uncle doctor this sick old cow. It took us all day. I didn't even have time to go to the movies. Did you go?"

"No."

"Why didn't you?"

"Because I hate to go to town."

"You never used to. You used to like to go to town. Even if we only had enough money for one bag of peanuts between us you used to like to." The strap around his books didn't look too strong but he took it by the end and swung it around and around. "Friday," he said, his grin buoyant. "I thought it'd never get here. Hey, Ellen Grae, I got me a new rod and reel. My uncle bought it for me. You want to meet me down at the river after a while and try it out?"

"I don't think so, Grover."

"Why not? School's out till Monday. You don't have to do homework tonight. Come on."

"I don't want to go down to the boat, Grover, and if you're going to walk the rest of the way home with me please shut up. You're making my head ache."

Grover stopped swinging the books and for five minutes he stopped talking. A car full of high school kids, giddy with Friday freedom, appeared in the dusty road, speeded past us and somebody threw out an empty Coke bottle. The sun, a scorching ball of white fire, breathing heat and sucking up the earth's moisture, touched the worn-out grass on both sides of the road. Heat waves danced on brown lace fences.

Grover squinted his eyes and looked up into the sun's glare and whistled a tune. He said, "They say a person's crazy if he can look right into the sun without scrooching up his eyes."

"Who says that, Grover?"

"Doctors. I read doctor books all the time. My uncle's got a whole room full of 'em."

"Has he?"

"He studied to be a doctor for humans before he decided that animals were more interesting. He says that animals are cleaner and that when people call other people animals it's a compliment. You should have seen him operate on that old sick cow last Saturday. Her sides were all bloated out about four feet and her eyes were all rolled back in her head and she was staggerin' around like she was drunk when we found her. We had a heck of a time getting her into the back seat of the car so's we could operate on her."

"You put a cow into the back seat of your uncle's car?"

"Well, no, come to think of it we didn't. We couldn't get her in. We had to do it right there on the ground. My uncle gave her a shot to knock her out and I grabbed my instruments and ran up to this farmhouse and boiled them, then I ran back and we put on our rubber gloves and operated. Ellen Grae, you should have seen . . ."

We had reached the McGruders' gate. "Grover," I said. "You'll have to tell me the rest of the story some other time. I'm home now."

"Wait a minute, Ellen Grae."

"So long, Grover. I'll see you."

"I got another real good story to tell you. I'll tell it real fast. We could go up on the porch and sit in the shade while I do it. It'll cheer you up. I don't know what's wrong with you but you look like you need cheering up."

"So long, Grover. I'll see you."

"All right," said Grover, scowling. He turned and humped off down the road and I turned and opened the gate and went up the walk and the steps and opened the screen door and stepped into the coolness of the house and there, sitting on Mrs. McGruder's chintz sofa, were Grace and Jeff.

✕✕✕

THEY STAYED AT the Gingham Inn the name of which, Grace said, was supposed to make people coming in at the train station two blocks away, think of comfortable rooms with braided rugs on the floors and red geraniums in window boxes and homey cleanliness.

"But it's the misnomer of all times," she declared, pulling back the sheets on her bed to better examine the mattress for bedbugs. "Did you remember to ask Mrs. McGruder for a clean fruit jar, Ellen Grae?"

"Yes, ma'am. She gave me two. What are they for?"

"To keep my nylons in. Roaches love nylon and this place is alive with the nasty things. I found that out last year. Since when," she asked, "has ma'am and sir become a part of your vocabulary?"

"I don't know. Since I came back here this time, I guess. I thought it sounded nicer than just answering yes and no."

Grace's eyes, keen and gray and sober, studied me. "You're a nice kid, Ellen Grae. It's too bad you couldn't have inherited some nice, normal parents."

"I think you and Jeff are nice, normal parents, Grace. I like you."

Grace said, "Thank you, dear. We don't deserve it but thank you."

"See any bedbugs?"

"I don't think so. Of course you never can tell until it gets dark. That's when they make their grand entrance." Her hands, without rings and lightly tanned, smoothed the sheets back into place, drew the counterpane. Turning, she said, "Well now, I think we can talk but I think your father should be present while we're doing it. You want to run down the hall and get him, honey? He's in room eighteen."

"What are we going to talk about?" I asked. "What's wrong?"

"We don't know, yet," she answered. "That's why we're here. To find out."

They had come to find out why I ate so much and yet grew skinnier all the time, and why I slept so much and yet was tired all the time, and why I cried in my sleep, and why my grades at school had turned from being A's into C's and why I refused to accompany Rosemary to the movies on Saturday afternoons.

They sat on chairs and I sat on the bed. There was the smell of Grace's clean cologne in the room and Jeff's after-shave lotion and stale furniture wax and molding carpet. There was the sound of water running through pipes and a loud, overhead radio voice. There was this feeling of airless closeness, like just before a storm.

While I was down the hall getting Jeff, Grace had changed her dark dress to a light one and put on fresh lipstick. Her brown hair, drawn back from her face and held with a velvet ribbon, was sweet. She and Jeff gave each other grave smiles. To me Grace said, "Now then, Ellen Grae."

"Ma'am?"

She crossed her beautiful legs. "It's really no use, you know, to put on that bland face with us. We've come to find out what's wrong and we're going to find out what's wrong if we have to sit here all night."

"And I don't want to sit here all night," Jeff said. "After we get our powwow out of the way I want the three of us to go out and find the best restaurant in town, and I want us to eat the best dinner they have to offer, and then I want to take you to the movies. We'll get a loge."

"There isn't anything wrong," I said. "You don't want me to invent something just to satisfy you, do you?"

Jeff examined the palms of his hands. "No, the truth will do. If you don't mind let's have it."

The water in the pipes hammered and the radio voice from the room above quickened to a rich, pleading insistence. At the window a lukewarm breeze stirred the weary curtains. The dream I had had of Ira wept against the walls of my mind.

I said, "There isn't anything wrong. Let's go eat. I'm going to have steak if you can afford it."

"Is it our being divorced?" they asked. "Are you having trouble with that at school?"

"No, I'm not having trouble with your being divorced at school. Is there any ice? Could I have a drink of water, please?"

Grace fixed me a drink of ice and water in a plastic cup. "Your father and I are still very good friends," she said. "And we always will be. You know that, don't you?"

"Yes, I know that."

"Are you worried about one of us re-marrying?"

"No. I think about it sometimes—I know that it might happen sometime but I'm not worried about it. I'm not worried about anything."

"Are you having trouble with Rosemary?" they asked.

"No, I'm not having any trouble with Rosemary. I like her better this year than I did last year even though she's still stuck-up but that isn't her fault. Her father makes her that way."

A smile dawdled at the corners of Jeff's mouth. "We understand you went hunting for lost treasure about three weeks ago."

"Yeah."

"Find anything?"

"Naaah."

"How's Grover?"

"Fine."

"You still like him, don't you?"

"Sure. Of course he's a terrible liar but that doesn't hurt anything. Grover's fine. I like him."

Grace took the ribbon out of her hair. Now there was the beginning of dusk in the room, softly creeping.

Grace pushed her hair back and again fastened the velvet ribbon. The bones in her face stood out suddenly, white and sharp. She said, "How's Ira?"

"Who?"

"Ira. The man who sells peanuts."

"Oh. You mean Ira."

"That's right. How is he?"

"I dunno. I reckon he's all right. He was the last time I saw him."

"And when was that?"

"That was . . . let's see . . . I reckon the last time I saw Ira was the day Grover and me went treasure hunting."

"Ira went with you, didn't he?"

"Yes, ma'am."

"And you haven't seen him since?"

"No, ma'am."

"You and he used to be pretty good friends, didn't you?"

"I reckon we did."

"But you're not anymore?"

"I didn't say that. I didn't say we weren't friends anymore. I just said I hadn't seen him since Grover and I took him treasure hunting with us."

"Mrs. McGruder told your father and me that you were the only person in town that Ira would talk to. What does he talk about?"

"Nothing. Missouri. He's got a goat and her name's Missouri. He talks to me about her sometimes."

"Has Ira ever said anything out of the way to you?"

"What do you mean?"

"Has he ever said anything wrong to you?"

"No. Ira's sweet. He wouldn't say anything wrong to anybody."

"Why are you sweating?"

"I'm not sweating."

"Yes you are. It's all over your face. Your face is covered with it."

"Well, I drink a lot of water and then I sweat. Why don't we go and eat now? I'm hungry, aren't you?"

"You're sweating because I'm questioning you about Ira. I want to know why, Ellen Grae, and if we have to sit here all night I'm going to find out."

"I'm not sweating because of Ira. I'm sweating because I'm hot."

"What did he say to you?"

"Nothing!"

"Are you sure?"

"Yes!"

Grace's own face was palely glistening. She leaned forward in her chair and spoke to me, slapping the words together, one by one. She said, "You talk about Ira in your sleep. Mrs. McGruder told us that she heard you talking about him in your sleep. Why?"

"I don't know why! I don't believe I do!"

"Mrs. McGruder wouldn't lie," Jeff said.

"I didn't say she lied! I just said . . . hell's afire, I don't know what I said!"

"Crying won't help," Jeff said. "And neither will swearing."

"I'm not crying! I'm not swearing! You're trying to twist me all up! You're trying to make me tell things about Ira that I don't want to tell!"

"What things about Ira don't you want to tell?"

"Nothing! I don't know anything about Ira I don't want to tell!"

"A minute ago you said you did. A minute ago you said we were trying to make you tell things about Ira that you didn't want to tell."

"Well, you are! Leave me alone. Quit picking on me."

"We're not picking on you. We're just talking. Tell us about Ira."

"What do you want to know about him?"

"What does he talk to you about?"

"I told you. He talks to me about his goat. Her name's Missouri."

"What else?"

"Nothing! That's all!"

"Why is it you don't like to come to town anymore?"

"Because I just don't like to. Is there anything wrong with that?"

"No, there's nothing wrong with it but we think there's another reason. Is it because you're afraid you might run into Ira?"

"Of course not!"

"You're lying, Ellen Grae."

"I'm not! I'm not!"

"What things about Ira don't you want to tell?"

"Nothing! It's a secret! Nobody knows except me!"

"Knows what?"

"It wasn't his fault! They tried to kill him first! He told me that! It wasn't his fault! They were pulling him through the swamp . . . and they had a rattlesnake in a box . . . and they were poking at the snake with a stick . . . trying to make it bite Ira . . . but instead it bit them . . . and . . . and . . . he said . . . they both swelled up and died . . . and they were so far back in the swamp . . . and he didn't know what else to do . . . and he buried them!"

A silence followed during which Jeff wound his watch. I thought he was never going to stop.

A sigh came into Grace's face. She said, "Oh, honey."

"It's the truth! I'm not making it up!"

Jeff looked at Grace. "Well, this one stumps me. A guy who isn't all there in the brains department, who never says a word to anybody except our daughter, tells her that he buried his parents out in the swamp after a snake bit them, and she's made herself sick over it."

"They'll put him in jail or the crazy house," I whispered. "And he'll die and it'll be my fault."

Jeff's question traveled over my head to Grace. "What do you think we ought to do?"

"He trusts me," I said. "I'm the only one he ever talks to. I'm not making this up. The day we went treasure hunting . . . and we got to this place in the swamp . . . I know they're there . . . they've been there all the time . . . years and years . . . but it wasn't Ira's fault . . . he didn't kill them . . . the snake did."

Jeff said, "All right, Ellen Grae. All right. I think we've got it all now."

"What are you going to do?"

They shook their heads and said, "We don't know. We'll do something but right now we don't know what."

※※※

I DIDN'T GO BACK to the McGruders' that night. After we ate some boxed fried chicken, which Grace sent out for, Jeff took a taxi and went out to the McGruders' and brought back some pajamas and other stuff for me.

I took a warm bath with some oil beads poured in the water.

We didn't talk any more about Ira.

About ten o'clock Jeff went to his room and Grace creamed her face and put on her pajamas and we went to bed.

No bedbugs bit us.

It stormed.

Early in the murky morning we rose and dressed and then Jeff came and we went to the drugstore for breakfast. While we were eating it Jeff talked about his work and Grace talked about her job. They both said they'd like to buy me a little present. "We thought maybe a ring like Rosemary's and a cute little gold wristwatch to match," they said. "Would you like that?"

My orange juice tasted like metal but I drank it anyway. "Thank you. That'd be nice."

Their smiles were easy and relaxed. "We forgot to ask you—how are things at school, Ellen Grae?"

"Fine. Just fine."

"No problems?"

"No. Mrs. McGruder helps me with my homework."

"What's your favorite subject this year?"

"English. I like words and stories."

Grace leaned and pulled a paper napkin from the metal holder on the table and fastidiously wiped her fingertips. "English was always my favorite subject too. And I just *loved* to write stories. What I created was always so real to me."

"Yes," I said, "what I create is always real to me too."

It was a delicious discovery. Grace hugged me.

Casually Jeff said, "How do you feel this morning?"

"Fine, thank you."

"Sleep all right?"

"Yes, sir. Did you?"

"Oh, I always sleep like a rock."

They were waiting for me. Their faces were bland but with little puddles of waiting in them. I said, "Looks like it's going to be a good day."

"Yes," they said. "It looks that way."

"We don't have to do anything, do we? We can just spend all day enjoying ourselves, can't we? We're not worried about anything, are we?"

Grace said she wasn't sure and Jeff started talking to me about moral responsibility. "Those are two fearful words," he said. "And a little girl your age should not be too concerned with them and yet you must be. You realize that, don't you, Ellen Grae?"

I said, "I might realize it if I knew what they meant. Of course I know what morals are and I know what responsibility means. When you put them together I'm not exactly sure what they mean."

Jeff added sugar to his black coffee. "Moral responsibility is what you feel toward Ira. You feel that a moral wrong has been committed and because you have a conscience you are troubled and concerned and distressed. Because you know about this wrong you feel responsible."

"Jeff," I said, "I feel a lot better about things today than I did yesterday."

"Naturally. We're here now and you've confided in us and some of the weight has been lifted from you."

"So why don't we just skip it?"

"Is that what you want to do? Skip it?"

"It probably isn't true what he told me."

"Do *you* think it's true?"

"Anyway, even if it is true it wasn't his fault."

Jeff said, "Yes, all of us here understand that."

"It happened a long time ago. Maybe before I was even born. I don't know why *I* should have to worry about it."

"You don't have to. There's no law that says you have to."

I put a hunk of toast in my mouth, chewed it, and swallowed it. It went down dry. "You don't think they'd put Ira in the crazy house, do you, Jeff?"

"I don't know, Ellen Grae."

"Or in jail?"

"I don't know what they'd do to him, dear. I doubt very much if he'd go to prison. I don't know Ira—he's never said one word to me. When I buy peanuts from him I hand over the money and he hands over the sack and that's all. But offhand, just judging from what I've seen, I'd say he isn't mentally responsible."

"He isn't mentally responsible and so I'm morally responsible."

"You are only if you want to be, Ellen Grae. You let your conscience decide what's to be done."

"I have to decide all by myself?"

"Well, you're the one who's been worried about it.

Grace and I haven't been. We didn't even know about it until yesterday."

"What would you do if you were me?"

"You know."

"I wish I was deaf," I said. "I wish he hadn't told me."

Jeff said, "Well, you aren't deaf and he *did* tell you. And now the question is, what are we going to do about it?"

"I don't see why I should be morally responsible for what somebody else has done."

"Your objection isn't an original one," Jeff said.

"Who would we have to go see?"

"The sheriff. Do you know him?"

"Only when I see him. His name's Irby Fudge. His office is right down the street."

Jeff bought me a pair of colored glasses before we left the drugstore. He said that they weren't to hide behind or cover up anything but that the sun looked like it was going to come out bright and hot and that I should get in the habit of wearing them, starting at once, to protect my eyes.

❊❊❊

SHERIFF FUDGE HAD a plump, open face and a wide, friendly smile that said he liked you on sight, whoever you were and whatever your mission was. This smile of his invited you to like him also but in it was the hope that you hadn't come to him with any real trouble. His favorite word was shucks but before he let us know that he said he was mighty glad to meet us. Were we, he inquired, any relation to the Derryberrys over in Pierce County?

Jeff said no, no relation.

Sheriff Fudge said that that was too bad. That the Pierce County Derryberrys were mighty fine people. Law abiding and peace loving and minders of their own business. He invited us to sit down but there weren't enough chairs to go around so he sat on the corner of his desk. He said that he had seen me around town with Grover and the McGruders. What, he asked, could he do for us?

Jeff said, "Well, our daughter here is worried about one of your citizens. She's told us quite a story about him and now she wants to tell you."

"All right," said Sheriff Fudge and settled himself more solidly.

I told him my story about Ira. And all the time I was telling it it was plain to see that he considered all of it some kind of a sadly funny joke.

When I finished with it and fell silent Sheriff Fudge smiled his broad smile, passed a hand over his short, burnished hair and said, "Shucks."

Jeff said, "I beg your pardon?"

"Shucks," Sheriff Fudge said grinning. "I beg *your* pardon, Mr. Derryberry, but if you could only know how silly your little girl's story sounds. Shucks. Ira's parents aren't buried out in the swamp. They ran off and left him years ago. They're up north."

"Where up north?" Jeff asked.

Sheriff Fudge's expression gently apologized for his ignorance. He said, "Well now, shucks, I don't know that. That's something I can't tell you. But they're up there and you can rest assured of that."

Jeff reached inside his shirt cuff and his fingers found his watch. He wound it and wound it.

Sheriff Fudge slid from his desk leaving a round, polished spot. He walked around it to the window and looked out. Then he came back and sat down again. His smile was big and patient. He said, "Mr. Derryberry, has Ira ever talked to you about anything?"

Jeff stopped winding his watch. "Well, no. Of course I don't know him. I don't live here. I only come once in a while to visit my daughter."

Sheriff Fudge's smile grew. "It wouldn't make any difference if you *did* know him—if you *did* live here. You'd still never get him to talk to you. He doesn't talk to anybody. He just looks and points."

A dark rose blush crept into Jeff's cheeks. "Ellen Grae says that Ira talks to her."

Irby Fudge's laugh was rich and languid. "Yes, I know what Ellen Grae says. I know all about her stories. Everybody in Thicket does."

Grace removed her white gloves and reached into her purse and withdrew a blue tissue but didn't use it for anything.

"My wife and I are friends with the McGruders," Sheriff Fudge explained. "We belong to the same church and my wife and Sally McGruder belong to the same bridge club."

"Mrs. McGruder is a wonderful person," Grace commented.

"They play every Wednesday night," Sheriff Fudge said. "Your little girl here provides the entertainment."

Jeff said, "What do you mean?"

"Story entertainment. Sally McGruder gets 'em from Ellen Grae and brings 'em to the bridge club and tells 'em. Then all the wives go home and the husbands hear 'em and everybody gets a good laugh. Don't you know about the stories your little girl tells?"

Jeff's face was stiff and embarrassed. "Yes, we know about them."

Grace put her gloves in her purse. She turned and looked at me.

I looked at Sheriff Fudge's plump leg with the shiny shoe on the end of it moving back and forth.

"Of course I wouldn't give you a nickel for a kid without imagination," Sheriff Fudge said in a kindly way.

I thought about Ira's mother and her husband. They must have been mean and ugly, big, wicked people with big, wicked thoughts and intentions.

Irby Fudge's foot looked comfortable in its soft, gleaming shoe. Above it the ankle was covered with an olive-colored sock, ribbed and very neat. I thought of Ira's feet which were shaped something like

Grace's; high arched and free of corns because he hated shoes and wouldn't wear them even when it was cold. Ira didn't like noise either except natural ones, like the sound of the river sweeping past his shack and the sound of the wind, high in the mighty trees and the way the ground sounds underfoot on a still, frosty morning, full of sharp cracks and squeaks. Thicket had a noon whistle and once I had seen Ira cover his ears and shake during its wailing shriek.

"But sometimes their little imaginations run away with them," Sheriff Fudge said.

A picture of Ira's mother and her husband as they must have been came stealing into my mind. They would have had raw faces, sour and furtive, with sly eyes and mouths that had been desecrated by all the evil that lay within them. Anybody who could put a rattlesnake in a box and poke at it with a stick in the hopes that it would stick its vile head out and bite and bring death to somebody else had to look that way.

Sheriff Fudge was still swinging his foot and looking at me, and Grace was still turned around in her chair looking at me, and so was Jeff.

Jeff said, "Well, Ellen Grae?"

I thought, well I *did* try. Nobody can say that I didn't try. Hell's afire.

Grace said, "Ellen Grae?"

I said, "Well it's true that I do make up stories once in a while and sometimes they do kind of get away from me. Get bigger as I go along."

"Was that tale you told your father and me about Ira last night a story?" Grace asked.

I hung my head. "Sort of. I guess I got carried away with it."

Jeff's eyes brimmed with a sudden, deep sadness. He said, "Well, my word."

I pretended that my neck didn't have any muscles in it. That way it let my head hang loose against my chest. "I'm sorry. It's just that . . . when I think about stories and work them all out in my mind they get so real. I'm sorry. I don't want to cause anybody any trouble or hurt anybody. It's just that . . . well, it *was* real to me."

From Jeff's stomach there came a watery sound like it had just turned over.

Sheriff Fudge's foot, swinging back and forth, looked gay almost.

I raised my head and looked at them. Sheriff Fudge's expression was amused, Jeff's was strained. Grace's lovely mouth was cool and so were her eyes. She said, "Oh, Ellen Grae, really. You disappoint me."

"I'm sorry," I whispered. "I'm really very sorry about the whole thing."

Sheriff Fudge's smile was luxuriant. It forgave me.

THEY WERE ANGRY. They went back to the Gingham Inn and packed up and went back to the city. I didn't get the promised watch and ring. Their good-bye kisses and hugs were not free and warm. They didn't look back and wave when their train pulled out of the station.

Mrs. McGruder was there and she put her arm around me and we stood there and watched until the last silver car, wriggling and swaying, had become a part of the misty distance. Then we walked back to where Mrs. McGruder had parked her car and got in it and drove around to the drugstore and each of us had a Black Cow which cost Mrs. McGruder a quarter apiece but she said she was feeling extravagant. She said she hoped I wouldn't vomit mine up because it had cream in it and would soothe my stomach.

I didn't vomit mine up.

We went home and Rosemary, her hair in curlers, with egg white smoothed on her face to deal with sagging muscles and impending pimples, showed me her new wig which had arrived from the mail-order house that morning. She looked like a lion in it but I didn't say so. I told her that I thought the tawny tresses, so artfully arranged, bestowed a presence to her face.

"What do you mean presence?" she asked, drawing a purple bow on her mouth with a lipstick brush.

"Presence. Some people's faces have presence and some have absence. Yours has presence with that wig on. If I were you I'd wear it all the time. Who moved my books, Rosemary?"

"I did. Mrs. McGruder told me to clean up this room this morning. Your half was filthy. I found three pairs of dirty socks under your bed. Honestly, Ellen Grae."

"Rosemary, just for the experience you should spend a night at the Gingham Inn sometime."

"No thanks. That place gives me the creeps just to walk by it."

"They have bedbugs in their mattresses. Have you ever seen a bedbug?"

"Of course not."

"The Gingham Inn has thousands of them. You know those little buttons they put on mattresses to hold them together?"

"Yes, Ellen Grae."

"That's where they hide until you turn out the lights and go to sleep. Under those buttons."

"God, it was peaceful here without you around," Rosemary said. She erased the first purple bow and started on a second. "Excuse me, I forgot to ask you how your parents were."

"They're fine."

"Is your father still living in his garret?"

"Yes. He's going to move out about Christmas time though."

"To another garret, I suppose."

"No, not to another garret. He's decided to give up being an artist and go to Europe and become a *guérisseur*."

"What for?"

"Because *guérisseurs* make a lot of money and artists don't."

Inexpertly Rosemary removed the second mouth. Her efforts left a livid stain. Her cheekbones and forehead and temples, covered with dried egg white, had taken on a strange glow. She said, "I've got some stuff to dye my eyebrows with but I suppose if I did it Mrs. McGruder would have a fit."

"He's going to live with this other very famous *guérisseur* on a houseboat in The Netherlands and take lessons from him."

"Cinnamon-colored eyebrows," Rosemary grieved, leaning forward to examine the pale sepia question marks. "I hate them."

"All of the kings and queens in Europe go to him to get healed. A maharaja gave him a beautiful diamond crown one time just for curing him of a rare bone disease that had wasted away one of his legs up to the knee."

Rosemary examined her tongue. Its appearance, very pink and very shiny, obviously pleased her. She said, "I can't stand people with coated tongues. It makes me sick to my stomach. Your friend Grover was here about an hour ago. He said to tell you he was going down to his boat and that in case you came home any time soon for you to come on down. Honestly, Ellen Grae, your choice of friends is really disgusting."

Poor Rosemary.

Mrs. McGruder didn't jaw at me when I asked her if I could go down to the river and spend an hour or so with Grover. She made me two peanut butter and jelly sandwiches and two tuna fish salad ones and wrapped up a dozen ginger snaps in waxed paper. She did it lovingly and I told her I appreciated it and for some reason her eyes filled up with tears. She said, "Oh, Ellen Grae."

"Ma'am?"

"Nothing. I'm just glad your parents didn't take

you away from me. However trying you may be at times you still add something to my life."

"You add something to my life too, Mrs. McGruder. You and Mr. McGruder. Say, where *is* Mr. McGruder?"

"He's gone to the bakery for me."

"I love bakeries. They always smell so good. I used to know this girl whose father owned one and every afternoon after school we'd stop in at it and he'd give us stuff. For my birthday he gave me a cake that looked like a telegram. Yellow with black writing on it that said happy birthday. He was a dear man and everybody said that he didn't deserve the kind of fate that befell him. Even though he had a devil's temper and beat on his car with a two-by-four every time it wouldn't start."

"He *sounds* like his temper might have been a little unruly," Mrs. McGruder commented.

"Don't you want to know what his fate was?"

"Yes. Tell me about it."

"His car threw a rod one day while he was beating on it because it wouldn't start and it pierced his liver and he died."

"The rod pierced his liver?"

"It impaled him. I saw the whole thing. He looked so shocked when it happened. This rod, pointed on the end like an arrow, shot out like lightning from the hood. Right through the metal. And it impaled him. He was Catholic and the priest came right away and said the last rites for him. I gave him my linen handkerchief. I think Catholics die so pretty, don't you?"

Mrs. McGruder added two flowered paper napkins to the sack which contained the sandwiches and the ginger snaps. "I think," she said, "that for a little girl who is as much concerned with life as you are that you are much too occupied with death. Here is your lunch and Godspeed. Be back here by two o'clock at the latest."

XXX

THE DAY WAS AT its most glorious hour. Dressed in gold and blue light it sparkled. The face of the sky was wide and tranquil. The flat, brown land, faintly damp from its bath of the night before, looked revived. There were clusters of quiet clouds. It was hot and still. I heard the rush of the river long before I reached it.

Grover was sitting in the boat with his fishing hat pulled down low over his eyes. I threw my shoes and the lunch down at him but he didn't move. The boat rocked with my weight when I followed the lunch and the shoes and climbed aboard but all he did was let out a big sigh.

I said, "Hey, what're you doing?"

"Nothin'. Just sittin' here waitin' for you. Where've you been?"

"Nowhere. Hey, how come you aren't out with your uncle learning how to be a veterinarian today?"

"He gave me the day off. You want to go fishin'?"

"I reckon I do. You dug the worms already?"

"I dug a few. Somethin's been at my worm bed. I'm gonna have to put some chicken wire up around it I guess. Why don't you sit down?"

"I *am* sitting down. What do you reckon it was after your worms?"

"I dunno. A dog maybe."

"Dogs don't eat worms. Only birds and fish eat worms."

Grover pushed his hat to the back of his head. He looked at me. "Ellen Grae, I don't think I'm gonna be a veterinarian."

"You don't? What's wrong?"

"Well, you know that old sick cow I helped my uncle operate on last Saturday?"

"Yes."

"Somebody—I guess it was me—left a piece of

towel in her. Yesterday the owner noticed the end of
it stickin' out of the incision and called my uncle
and my uncle had to go over there this morning and
take it out."

"Oh, Grover, that's terrible. But you couldn't help
it, could you?"

"Sure I could have but I didn't. I don't know how it
happened except that I guess I was pretty excited. My
first operation and all."

"Grover, it could have happened to anybody."

"No it couldn't have. It could only have happened
to me. My uncle's right—I'm clumsy."

"I don't think you're clumsy. I think you're very
graceful."

"Ellen Grae, I don't want to be graceful. I just don't
want to be clumsy."

"Well, it's the same thing. If you're not clumsy you
have to be graceful. That's the way the world is,
Grover, and you might as well accept it."

"Okay, I'll accept it," Grover said, his face full of
red irritation. He reached and pulled his oar from its
lock. "If we're gonna go fishin' let's get goin'. Which
way you want to go? Up the river or down?"

"Down will be all right. But I only want to go as
far as the bend."

"I'll be lucky if that cow doesn't get gangrene,"
Grover muttered. He stood up, pulled his stomach in
and then let it out again, removed his hat and then
put it on again, sucked in his cheeks. "You can shove
us off any time you get ready," he said, his eyes
melancholy.

I shoved us off and we paddled out into the middle
of the stream and headed downward. The river,
chestnut-hued and spangled with patches of sun, received us smoothly. The wind was warm and courte-
ous. Banners of gray moss swung without excitement from the trees on both banks. A bird's cry, loud
and high but without alarm in it, pierced the air.

"Isn't it pretty out here?" I asked Grover. "See how
pretty it is?"

He said, "Yeah, it's all right. I seen it before. Why are you rowin' so fast?"

"I'm not rowing fast. I'm just rowing. Do you want to stop and fish?"

"Naw, I don't think so. I don't feel like fishin' today."

"Grover," I said. "You'll feel better about things after a while. What you've got to do is put that cow out of your mind. When bad things happen to me that's what I do. I just put them out of my mind."

"How do you do that?"

"I just do it. Think about something else. That's what I do."

"Yeah," Grover said, hefting his paddle with new energy. "Yeah."

"You still know how to write poetry, Grover?"

"I dunno. I only wrote that one about the monk and I forgot how it goes."

"I'll bet if you tried to write another one you could. That'd take your mind off of the cow. Why don't you try it?"

"You mean now?"

"Sure. You're not doing anything else. Write a poem; it'll make you feel better."

"What about?"

"Grover, I don't know what to tell you to write about. Write about anything. Write about fish or birds or us out here having a good time."

"We're at the bend," Grover informed me. "You want to turn around and go back now?"

"In a minute. I just want to see if I can see Ira. Is that him out there hanging up clothes?"

Grover grinned for the first time that day. "No, that's Missouri. That's Ira over there by the trash pit eatin' paper."

I stood up in the boat and hollered and waved to Ira. With something white in his hand he turned from the line and waved back. Missouri lifted her head from whatever it was in the trash pile she was eating. Ira beckoned to her and she trotted over and stood beside him. He knelt and pointed to the boat and she leaned against him.

"You want to put in and visit him for a few minutes?" Grover asked.

"No. No, I just wanted to make sure he was all right. We can go on back now."

"Ira's nice," Grover remarked. "You're nice too, Ellen Grae. You always make me feel better about things."

His compliment uplifted me but kind of sorrowed me too—brought a loneliness. For who was going to make *me* feel better about things? For just a second a pang of self-pity smote me but then I thought, Oh, hell's afire, Ellen Grae, you *wanted* to save Ira. Nobody made you. So quit your bellyaching. Maybe a way to make yourself feel better will come to you tomorrow, or the next day or the next. Something will come to you; it always does. Think positive.

I lifted my oar and helped Grover maneuver the boat around for the homeward journey.

Grover said, "You're a good sailor, Ellen Grae."

"Thank you, Grover. So are you."

We both laughed.

On the way back up the river, with me in the bow and Grover in the stern, Grover thought of a poem he could write to take his mind off the cow.

"It's about you," he said. And recited it to me:

> ON THE RIVER AND AWAY FROM THE COW
> AND ELLEN GRAE IS SITTIN' IN THE BOW.
> WE'VE LEFT THE RIVER BEND BEHIND NOW.
> SO LONG, IRA. GOOD-BYE, COW.

LADY ELLEN GRAE

Chapter 1

BEING A NORMAL PERSON I am not beset with a lot of superfluous anxieties and apprehensions. I do not borrow from yesterday or tomorrow. I live for the day I am in and I like it to start early the way it did on this particular day.

The beginning was nice and average. I got up early, the way I always do, and looked out. Everything looked the way it usually did. It was dry and still. A butterfly, the color of deep flamingo, clung blindly to the screen door. I brushed its wingtips with my finger and it jerked itself free and flew away.

I took my cold breakfast from a jar and sat down to eat it.

The morning paper wasn't very juicy. Two criminally insane patients from the state hospital at Chattahoochee had escaped and were at large. The governor needed more money to run the state of Florida but didn't know where he was going to get it. Growers throughout the citrus belt were worried about the drought. A man in Jacksonville had been granted a divorce from his harridan wife because she scrubbed a pair of his filthy shoes with his toothbrush, then put the brush back in its usual place, and he used it and got a gum infection and all of his teeth fell out. A department store in Tampa was having a sale—foam rubber pillows, two for five dollars. A court judge, sentencing a woman to life imprisonment for the murder of her husband, had declared that women have simply got to stop killing their husbands.

About six thirty Jeff joined me for his kind of breakfast: two hot eggs, a piece of cremated toast, and coffee. With a thready look he viewed the bones and gristle left over from my pickled pig's foot, but then his face gentled and his wonderful smile spread and he said, "Well, Ellen Grae, I see you're all girded up for the day."

"Yes, sir, I'm all prepared for it."

"You and Grover going fishing?"

"We thought we might. We didn't catch anything yesterday. You know something, Jeff? I think reporters are lazy."

Jeff incised one of his eggs and the yolk ran out, a nauseating sight. "What reporters?"

"The reporters that write this paper. This one says that yesterday morning the Honorable Judge John Jackson declared that women simply have got to stop killing their husbands."

With preparatory gusto Jeff gilded the white part of the ruptured egg with the yellow. "What's lazy about that? I heartily agree with the judge. Women *should* stop killing their husbands. In fact he might have stretched his point a little and said that people should stop killing people."

"Oh, I agree with you, Jeff, but that's not what I'm talking about. I'm talking about a reporter who wrote this story."

Jeff incised his other egg and its yolk poured out to meet the first one. "What about him?"

"Well, this lady by the name of Pansy Dugger killed her husband last Christmas Day. He didn't remember it was Christmas and so she took her sawed-off shotgun and shot him five times. It must have been a terrible mess, him lying there where the first blast felled him with his life's blood gushing out of him, his eyes rolled back in his head, froth on his lips, his limbs twitching."

A muscle in Jeff's cheek jerked. He gazed at his

eggs. "Well, he probably had it coming to him and more. Did you say you and Grover were going fishing?"

"Yes, sir. He'll be here in a few minutes. Where was I? Oh, yes. In the corner of their little, humble cabin cowered Dingo, their mangy old dog. Dingo didn't like Pansy killing his master because he could remember all the good times they had had together out possum hunting in the woods and so about the third time Pansy pulled the trigger he bared his fangs and sprung on her. Pansy whirled around and blew his head off and there lay the dog and his master, both of them mortally wounded. I can just see it, can't you, Jeff?"

Though they didn't require it Jeff sawed at his eggs with his knife and fork. "Yes, but I'm trying not to. It's going to be a nice day, isn't it?"

"Yes, sir, it is. And just about that time some strolling carolers came up and started singing *Peace on Earth, Good Will Toward Men* and Pansy went out and gave them each a tangerine and a kumquat. She wasn't as cruel and stingy as people thought she was. Pansy Dugger. Has kind of a silky sound to it, hasn't it? But anyway, all this reporter says about the whole thing is that Pansy killed her husband and that yesterday, before the judge sentenced her to life imprisonment, he declared that women have simply got to stop killing their husbands. Looks to me like the reporter who wrote this is lazy. If it had been me writing it, I'd have made it real gory and shuddery. People like to read gory, shuddery things. And I'd have made it sentimental, too, so that people would cry when they read it. I'd have described the little pink angel on top of the Christmas tree, put there by Pansy's husband the night before. And maybe Pansy shedding a tear or two after her crime was done. Everybody likes to read about stuff like that. I wonder why that is."

Jeff, who is a neat eater, smiled at me and neatly ate a piece of his egg. "I don't know but to get this subject out of the way, if Pansy's husband put a little pink angel on top of their Christmas tree the night before she shot him, then it must have been apparent to her that he knew Christmas had arrived. Pansy doesn't sound like such a savory character to me. If I had been the judge I'd have ordered her guillotined. What kind of a dog was poor old Dingo?"

"Oh, I reckon he was just a dog."

"Doesn't the newspaper account say?"

"No, sir, they don't even mention him. That's another thing I've got against reporters. It isn't honest the way they cheat you out of details. If it had been me writing this I'd have described Dingo right down to his toenails. He was a beautiful light tan with a white belly and a white tip on his tail. When he came to America from Australia he couldn't bark but Mr. Dugger taught him how. Dingoes are strange dogs; they can't bark unless they're taught. All they can do is yelp and howl. In his time Mr. Dugger's Dingo was a fierce kangaroo hunter. There were lots of interesting things about him but that lazy reporter didn't even mention him. Well, that's the way the world is today. Everybody's in such a sweat and a push and shove all the time. I swear I don't know what for. You want to hear something interesting, Jeff?"

"Yes," replied Jeff with an agitated look. "Anything. Anything to get away from Pansy and Dingo."

"Grover and I were out at the cemetery yesterday afternoon looking at the headstones and we counted thirteen with the name of Younce. Grover said that most of them died from having migraine headaches caused from being in such a push and a shove all the time. All of them had three or four jobs. I remember the old grandfather, poor thing. You know he lived right down the road from the McGruders and people said they could smell his death coming long before it got here. I couldn't. He always smelled like talcum powder to me. People were afraid of him because he had outlived all the rest of his family and talked kind of strange. He said that when the time came he was going to joyfully fling the dust of this earth aside and ride up naked to the sweet airs of heaven. That's the way he talked and it scared people. You know Ralph down at the barbershop? Well, one day I was over at Mr. Younce's house reading to him and Ralph came to give Mr. Younce a haircut and you know what he told Ralph? That we were all made out of naught but clay and that the Great Potter would someday lead us all up the dark stairs to a door which no one had ever seen through or returned from and we'd all be pushed through it and then the Great Potter at His Wheel would grind us all up and return us all to the earth and make more clay out of our bodies. It scared Ralph so that he ran away without giving Mr. Younce his haircut. Mr. Younce just laughed and got out his clippers and cut his own hair. He could tell the most sadly pretty stories. He gave me his gold signet ring before he died. Did I ever show it to you, Jeff?"

On his plate Jeff's eggs had congealed. He looked at them and then at me. "No, but never mind going to the trouble now. I believe you. I think."

I said, "Oh, it's no trouble, Jeff," and skipped down to my room and got the ring from the box I kept it in and brought it back and showed it to him. "It's 18-karat gold, Mr. Younce told me. It's got papers."

Jeff took the ring in his palm, turning it so that the light glinted on its flat, engraved surface. "What kind of papers?"

"Papers saying that he was sound of mind and body when he gave it to me and that it's legally mine. Isn't it pretty, Jeff?"

"Yes, it's very handsome. How would you like to pour me some more coffee? I seem to have run out here."

I got up and poured him some more coffee. "I didn't go to his funeral because he asked me not to. He said he couldn't stand the way people squalled and blubbered at funerals. He said he was going to a place where the entertainment was a lot better than it is here and there wasn't anything to bawl about."

Jeff handed the ring back to me, pushed his eggs aside, and attacked his toast, cutting it into small, precise squares. Some shadows in his face appeared, strangely intense, heightened by the outlines of his bones and the color of his eyes. "Ellen Grae, I talked to your mother on the phone last night."

"Did you, Jeff? I hope you remembered to give her my regards. Grace is so nice. I think you and she are so civilized. Some divorced people aren't, you know. There's another girl in my class at school whose parents are divorced and she says all they do is gripe and haggle. She's the most wretched little human being I ever met. Well, she's not so little either. She weighs a hundred and sixty pounds because she has this nervous compulsion to eat all the time. Her mother's the same way so her father put a padlock on the refrigerator door. That's why they got the divorce."

Jeff reconsidered his eggs, drew his plate toward him again, smeared egg yolk on one of the toast squares, tucked it into his mouth, chewed, and swallowed. "Ellen Grae?"

"Sir?"

"I started out to tell you that I talked with your mother last night and that we've made a decision concerning you."

"Concerning me, Jeff?"

Jeff smeared another toast square but didn't eat this one. He turned his attention to his coffee. He said, "Now, Ellen Grae, you're eleven years old."

"Yes, sir, I know I am but I don't regret it. Have you ever noticed, Jeff, how some people regret their ages? The old ones want to be young and the young ones want to be old. I swear I don't see why people just can't be satisfied with the way they are. I am."

Jeff already had too much sugar in his coffee but he added more. "That's the trouble in a nutshell.

You're satisfied with the way you are but your mother and I are not."

"You're not, Jeff? What's wrong?"

The silver in Jeff's eyes was the color of old pewter. "Well, there are a number of things. In the first place you're completely uninhibited."

"Uninhibited. Yes, sir, I reckon I am but—"

"Your hair is unbelievable and your clothes are impossible and the condition of your room is shocking," said Jeff, and took a long swig of his syrupy coffee. "Then there are your lies."

"My lies. Oh, you mean my stories, don't you? Well, I admit that I sometimes tell those but I only do it to amuse myself and other people. I didn't know that you didn't want me to tell them, Jeff. I can stop telling them right away if you want me to. It might be a good idea for me to do it anyway, even if you don't want me to. Now, what else, Jeff?"

Jeff breathed the way he does when he can't get one of his paintings right. Two long breaths and one short one. "Ellen Grae, do you remember your Aunt Eleanor?"

"Yes, sir, I surely do. She has red hair and lives in Seattle. Her husband died while he was trying to climb that big mountain they've got out there. I remember the last time she came to visit us. I was four—no, maybe I was five. Anyway I remember. She gave me a string of beads. I still have them. Is she coming to visit us again, Jeff?"

Jeff breathed again, this time three short ones and one long one. "Yes, she's coming down again. This time Laura's coming with her."

"Laura? Oh. Oh, yes, my little cousin. Well, I'll try to make them as comfortable as possible while they're here. I'll get Grover to help me clean the house up. I can't get to it today because I've already made other plans but there's no hurry about it, is there?"

Jeff picked up his coffee spoon and examined it like he'd never seen one before. "Oh, no, there's no hurry about it. It'll be a couple of days before they get here." He returned the spoon to his saucer. "I'm going to Sarasota this morning. Probably won't be back before five this afternoon. Did you say you were going fishing with Grover?"

A warning sense in my head hoisted a black banner. "Yes, but maybe I'll change my mind. With Aunt Eleanor and Laura coming and all maybe I should stay here and work. Jeff, you said that you and Grace had made a decision concerning me but you didn't tell me what it was."

Again Jeff became acutely interested in the coffee spoon. "Oh, yes. I'm glad you reminded me." The spoon in his slender artist's fingers dripped one latent drop and then was subjected to a vigorous paper-napkin polishing. "Ellen Grae?"

"Sir?"

"Your mother and I have decided that you should go back to Seattle with your Aunt Eleanor when she goes."

"I beg your pardon, Jeff?"

"And go to school there this coming term."

"*Me? Me go to school in Seattle?* But Jeff, that's thousands of miles away from Thicket! That's way up near Alaska! Aw, you're just kidding me."

With eyes intent and bones suddenly glistening and mouth straight across, Jeff said, "No. No, Ellen Grae, I'm not kidding you." He gathered his breakfast dishes and carried them to the sink and wasted two quarts of hot water rinsing them.

His becalmed attitude made me want to screech but we Derryberrys are not demonstrative people so I didn't. I said, "Jeff, you don't have to rinse your dishes. I'll wash yours and mine up all at the same time in just a few minutes. In fact, I think I'll give the whole kitchen a good cleaning this morning."

Jeff turned off the hot water, dried his hands on a piece of paper toweling, turned and looked at me. "Ellen Grae."

"Sir?"

"This isn't something that just occurred to your

mother and me yesterday or the day before. We've been thinking about it for a long time."

"Yes, sir. I know you and Grace don't do things on the spur of the moment. I wasn't thinking of that."

"I know, to you, it seems a little sudden but everything has to have a beginning, doesn't it?"

"Yes, sir, I reckon it does but Seattle's clear at the other end of the United States! Hell's afire!"

Jeff winced like he always does when I forget and cuss, but remained steady. "You've had lots of beginnings in your life. By now you should know how to handle them."

"Yes, I know how to handle beginnings, Jeff. But . . . well, a strange environment so far away from everything I hold dear might do something horrendous to me mentally! Jeff, you and Grace . . . well, I'll just bet you haven't thought about all the facets in this case. I'm not questioning your judgment or anything like that but—"

"Ellen Grae."

"Sir?"

"Believe me, we've deliberated every facet in the case and it is our considered judgment that you should go to Seattle and live with your aunt for a while."

"Why?"

"Because your mother and I are unable to give you the kind of home life that you should have, and your aunt will do this."

"I have a home life here. Mr. and Mrs. McGruder make a wonderful home for me when I live with them."

"Mr. and Mrs. McGruder are like putty in your hands and you know it," said Jeff. "I'm not saying that they aren't good people, now, so you don't need to look at me like that. Grace and I are as fond of them as you are but you will have to admit that they do give you a lot of leeway."

"Jeff, they don't give me *any* leeway. Last winter Mrs. McGruder made me learn to like collards and you know how much I hate them and she never lets me stay up past nine o'clock and she jaws at me all the time about my clothes and taking baths. Well, not *all* the time. Most of the time I remember about clothes and baths by myself, due to her influence, but she still does it because . . . well, you know how she is."

Jeff took some more breaths and looked at his watch. "Yes, I know how Mrs. McGruder is and I know how you are. It's not exactly your fault. Grace and I are partially to blame. But you know, when you've made a mistake and realize that you've made one, you have to do the best you possibly can with what's left over, don't you?"

Sometimes it's best to agree with people even when you don't. It stops them from pressing and gives you time to think.

So I agreed with him then and he said we'd talk about it some more but that he had business in Sarasota first, and went out and got in his car and started the engine. "You'll get used to the idea," he said with a look of callous cheer. "By the time I get back from Sarasota this afternoon you'll be used to it. It's simply a matter of mental reconciliation."

"Sure, Jeff. Don't worry about me. I'm all right."

Relieved, he drove off into the morning sun and I went back into the house and contemplated things.

It's true, I've found, that most things are simply a matter of mental reconciliation, because the mind is elastic—it stretches and can be pulled this way and that. The trick is not to flinch from it. If you do you're a goner before you even get started. Mentally, I've reconciled myself to a thousand things: school, being a girl, collard greens, baths, the Methodist church even though I'm a Pantheist, the girl I have to share a room with when I live with the McGruders, lots of things.

But Seattle? Oh, no. No, sir. I, Ellen Grae Derryberry, do not reconcile to things like Seattle. I like it here and here I intend to stay until it's time for me to hop into my grave.

Chapter 2

THIS TOWN OF THICKET where I live with the Mc-
Gruders, a dear, sweet couple, during the school
year, only has fences for looks and locks on doors for
those few who live here who are not native. For
there is no crime in Thicket. It has a watchful sheriff
by the name of Irby Fudge who keeps the peace without using his gun, four brisk churches, and one post
office. There is a main street with sidewalks which
undulate and make unapologetic detours around the
trees which shade the store fronts. At noon the town
clerk presses a button in his office and a whistle atop
the fire station blows to let everybody know it's
lunch time. Day after sunny day and night after
starlit night Thicket is as neat and as beautiful as a
rose garden.

I love Thicket and everybody in it, even Grover,
though were I to tell him this he would run like a
preyed rabbit. Right after Jeff left that morning he
arrived. Usually he will immediately champion my
causes even when he doesn't understand them but
that day he dawdled. He said, "Well, Ellen Grae, if
you're going to take what's wrong, point by point,
you got to admit that your father's right about
your room. Of course I don't look in it every time
I come over here. Maybe it's changed some since the
last time I saw it?"

"No, Grover, it hasn't changed. It doesn't need to
change. I admit that it gets a little disarranged sometimes but it certainly isn't shocking."

"What's uninhibited?" Grover asked.

"Oh, hell's afire, Grover. Don't you know anything? Why don't you look up words when you don't know what they mean like I do? Uninhibited is when a person doesn't have any inhibitions."

Bright sunlight, streaming in through the open window touched Grover's brown, bony face. He reached inside his shirt and scratched his stomach, a habit which drives me crazy when I've got a problem to solve. Your eyes are glassy," he said. "Maybe you're sick. If you're sick your father wouldn't make you go to Seattle, would he?"

"Grover, I'm not sick. There isn't a thing wrong with me."

"Last week you said there was. Last week you said your blood pressure was 215 over 180. I told my uncle that and he said you should be in a hospital."

"Grover, that was last week. Everybody has high blood pressure at some time or other. Anything can cause it. Your uncle's a veterinarian; you should know that. Mine was caused from an embryo in my bloodstream. It's dissolved since. Now I'm fine."

Searching the situation for a consoling scrap Grover turned a brown, sorrowful gaze on me. "Seattle's where they have all the big salmon."

"Grover," I said. "I don't care what they have in Seattle. I'm *not* going out there with Aunt Eleanor. I just know that if I do I'll never get back. If it was you being threatened with a thing like this, I'd help you think of a way out. Help me."

"If you'd just tell me what uninhibited means," Grover said.

"Some other time, Grover. Don't bother me with things like that now. I've got to think. You know something? I'm not going to let it happen. There are ways out of things. I've been in some bad fixes before and always got out of them. Listen, do you think you could give me a home permanent?"

"Sure. Why not? All you do is wrap up hunks of hair on those roller things they use and then squirt it with that pink stuff that comes in the box and it comes out kinks. I've seen my aunt do it to her hair hundreds of times."

"Have you got money?"

"Maybe I've got about four dollars," Grover answered with a frugal look.

"You'll have to lend it to me. I need it to buy one of those home permanent-wave kits. You'll have to go and get it for me, too. Get the cheapest kind they've got and come straight back."

Grover sighs a lot. He sighed and said, "You think that just a permanent wave is going to make everything right that's wrong, Ellen Grae? Your hair's just one of the things. What're you gonna do about the others?"

"Grover, are you going to help me or not?"

"Yes, I'm going to help you. What do you want me to do?"

"Go and get me the home permanent kit. And while you're at it bring back three or four cardboard boxes."

"What do you need boxes for?"

"To pack some stuff in. Magazines and stuff I've been saving."

Grover's uncle, who studied to be a medical doctor before he changed his mind and became a veterinarian, has a lot of books on medicine and psychiatry and Grover is always reading them. He thinks he knows all about human behavior. One time he gave me a Rorschach test and just because I said that the ink splotch looked like a woman chopping down a tree he said I'd probably murder somebody before my life was out. "It's in the genes," he declared, his red and white smile filled with mystery. "Probably somewhere way back in your family there was insanity. You won't be able to help yourself when it happens."

Grover is a fatalist. He thinks that everything that happens is destiny. One time we were out in his rowboat on the river and this hurricane came up and if it hadn't been for me both of us would surely have drowned. The sky, which had been blue when we started out turned a queer, mustard yellow and from the trees on both sides of the riverbanks the birds started to screech and squawk and flap. The water beneath us started to heave and the wind, hot and heavy, lowered itself from the sky and took hold of us and lifted. It was the queerest, most terrifying experience of my entire life. I slid to one end of the boat and Grover slid to the other and we went way up in the air on a peak of angry, churning water and then slammed down into the swirling trough.

Grover didn't do a thing. I screamed at him to let me have his pants to make a sail out of but he just sat there calmly viewing the whole thing. Finally I whipped off my own pants—well, actually they were a pair of Jeff's whacked off to fit me—knotted them around one of the cane poles we had, hoisted it, and when the wind had filled both legs we were blown out of the eye of the thing. While all of this was happening Grover banged his head on the bait bucket and suffered a brain concussion which caused him to have a complete loss of memory. He said that if it really happened it was destiny. This was after I had resuscitated him, removing about a gallon of water from his lungs.

The hurricane blew itself out about a mile down the river and I put Jeff's pants back on and things quieted. Grover, with a dazed, pale look, sat up and said, "No, I don't remember a thing. It must have been destiny."

I have saved Grover's life three or four times and that's all he ever says about it—that it's destiny.

Grover is such a strong believer in invincible fate that he said there was no use in my even *trying* to foil Jeff's plan to ship me out to Seattle to live with Aunt Eleanor.

He knows that I have a lot of spirit; that I thrive on adversity, just like the rest of the Derryberrys, but still he said that.

By two o'clock that afternoon my head was a mess of wiry, spiral curls, brown and stiff, and Grover and I were both exhausted. I set the kinks, coaxing them into a frame of water-soaked ringlets and then we cleaned my room. Grover, with a set look, crawled under my bed and pushed all the stuff out with the broom. We packed some of it in boxes and stored it in the utility room and took the rest down to the river and burned it.

"It smells," Grover observed. "It's a wonder to me you didn't have some kind of toxic condition, breathing all that mildew."

Grover is one of those persons who always looks at the pessimistic side of things. His favorite part of the newspaper is the obituaries and he's always talking about bacteria and impurities and diseases. One summer he worked for his uncle and came out of that experience knowing quite a bit about animals and their illnesses but he says that human mental weaknesses are going to be his chosen field when the time comes. He claims that nobody is as strong mentally as they are physically.

"Take you," he said, his dark eyes patched with anxiety. "Now, I think you might be able to outsmart your aunt and your father for a few days physically but mentally I don't think you'll be able to do it. That's where they'll catch you—mentally."

"For a person who doesn't even know what uninhibited means that's certainly a renowned statement, Grover."

"I looked uninhibited up while you were taking a bath," he reported sadly. "Now I know what it means. But anyway, Ellen Grae, I don't think you're strong enough to change yourself mentally overnight. All my uncle's books say this takes a long time. You don't need to sneer," he said rubbing his hands, that were all puckered from the permanent-wave lotion, up and down on the front of his shirt. "People who write those kind of books are professors and teachers. It takes them a long time to find out about things like that. The only way to change your personality in a hurry, they say, is to have a prefrontal lobotomy."

"What's that?"

"It's an operation they perform on the front lobes of your brain."

"What do they do that for?"

"Oh, to cure brain diseases."

"Grover, I don't have a brain disease."

"I know that but just let me finish. There are a lot of side effects to having a prefrontal lobotomy besides curing any brain disease you might have. Neat people that have one of these operations usually get sloppy afterward and sloppy people get neat afterward. There isn't much to it. All they do is run a thing that looks like an ice pick into your—"

"Grover, I give you my word that Jeff would never consent to me having my brain operated on even if I was insane. Anyway there isn't time. Aunt Eleanor and Laura will be here in a couple of days."

"Who's Laura?" Grover wanted to know.

"She's my cousin. She's thirteen years old. I don't know her very well. Just through Christmas cards and stuff like that but I must have told you about her some time or other."

"Oh, yeah," Grover said, watching me. "The girl who got attacked by a pack of wild dogs and had her lips chewed off. I remember now."

It was the time for a sober searching of my soul. I went to the sink and drew two glasses of tap-warm water and gulped them down and then I said, "Grover, you know I've got to change now and do it in a hurry and you've got to help me. Unless you want me to go to Seattle with Aunt Eleanor, that is."

"I don't want you to go to Seattle, Ellen Grae. I want you to stay here."

"All that stuff I told you about those wild dogs attacking Laura I just made up, Grover."

"You did?"

"Yes. What really happened was a squirrel bit her on her thumb."

"Did she get sick from it?"

"No. It wasn't rabid. Grover, from now on I've got to tell the whole, raw, absolute truth about everybody and everything and what I want you to do is hang around as much as possible and make sure that I do it. Stop me every time I start to tell a story."

Grover looked gloomy. "I like your stories. Everybody does."

"Jeff doesn't. He thinks I'm just a plain old liar."

Grover sighed. "Ellen Grae, I got a feeling that you're not going to get out of this one. I've just got a feeling. But you know I'll help you all I can. You know you can depend on me. Seattle," he said with one of his most dire looks. "It might as well be Siberia."

Grover *can* be sweet.

About five o'clock Jeff came home, hot and tired from his day of painting somebody's portrait. For our supper he had brought a cold, barbecued chicken and a carton of potato salad. He lavishly complimented me on the new hair style, admired the dress I was wearing, and took note of the unusual sight of my feet encased in shoes. He made a trip to the bathroom and on the way back stopped in at my room for a long look. "What happened to the floor?" he wanted to know.

"Grover oiled it. We couldn't find any wax. Doesn't it look nice? I remember how fussy Aunt Eleanor is. I'm going to let her and Laura have my room while she's here and I'll take the sun porch. I want their visit to be comfortable."

Jeff let his eyes rest on my wire curls. "Your mother and I have made up our minds, Ellen Grae. You're going back to Seattle with your Aunt Eleanor when she goes."

"Yes, sir. You told me that this morning and I'm all resigned to it. Should we eat on the porch, Jeff? It'll be cooler out there."

The chicken wasn't stringy and the potato salad

wasn't mushy but neither of us ate much. We talked about my going away.

"A whole new way of life is going to open out for you," said Jeff.

"Yes, sir. I've been thinking about it all day."

"Change isn't anything to be feared."

"No, I know it isn't. I'm not afraid."

"Seattle is a beautiful place. Someone has called it the Queen City of the Northwest."

"That sounds pretty."

"It's built on seven hills, like Rome, and is surrounded with water and mountains."

"Seven hills. Imagine that."

Jeff sighed. "I think your mother and I owe you some kind of an apology, Ellen Grae."

"No, you don't. It's not your fault that I'm like I am. But you know what I've been thinking, Jeff?"

"No. What?"

"That I could change here easier than I could in Seattle. I could ask Mr. and Mrs. McGruder to help me. And Grover. They know me; they'd do it. Of course I'd have to do most of it myself, I realize that. But I'm just saying that it would be a lot easier here than in strange surroundings, and having strange people trying to help me. You see what I did today. Didn't I make a good start today?"

Jeff rose and stood looking down at me. In his voice there was this tumble of regret and hope, of wary pessimism and warier cheer, all rabbled. "Yes," he agreed, "you made a good start today but it isn't just the things that you changed today that we're after. We're after the big values and your mother and I think you need some help with those."

I looked at the night, so beautiful with the mists rising up from the river and the voices from the swamp on the other side calling to each other like spirits. I tried but couldn't think of anything else to say and presently Jeff went inside to read and I continued to sit there, looking at the moon and the night clouds coursing across the face of it, until bedtime.

And I wasn't my own person any more and I was afraid.

Chapter 3

Two DAYS LATER Aunt Eleanor and Laura flew from Seattle to Tampa but from there had to take a train. It arrived, only six minutes late, and my aunt and cousin, clutching their train cases and ribboned hats, emerged from its air-conditioned intestine and disembarked.

Jeff stepped forward and embraced them both; Aunt Eleanor embraced him back and then me. She turned back to Jeff and grasped his hand and looked deep into his eyes and said, "You look so much like our father did." And tears came into her eyes.

Laura, in a pink sharkskin suit and pink shoes with black, grosgrain bows, handed me her train case. "Mother's so emotional," she commented. "Where's your car? Goodness, it's hot. Is it always this hot here? Aren't you afraid to let your skin get so brown? My good-grooming book says the sun is bad for your skin. I might like to get a light tan while I'm here but I certainly don't want to get as brown as you are."

The train case was heavy and the bottles and jars it contained clinked against each other as we walked across the concrete apron toward Jeff's car. The sun was savage, a blazing basketball. The still, afternoon air was like melted jelly.

We reached the car; I opened the back door and Laura climbed in ahead of me and settled herself on the hot, plastic seat. "It smells," she complained.

I set her train case on the floor. "It's just paint. Jeff hauls his paintings and stuff around in it."

Laura fanned herself with her hat, twisted a button until it fell off in her hand, and dabbed at her moist face with her handkerchief. "I've never been so hot," she declared. "What's keeping them so long? We didn't have *that* much luggage. I just hate trains but we couldn't get a plane from Tampa on. Have you a swimming pool?"

"No, but the river's right in back of our house. Grover and I swim in that."

"Grover? Who's Grover?"

"He's a friend."

"Your boy friend?"

"Well, he's a boy."

"Is he good-looking?"

"Not very."

"I don't like ugly boys," Laura said. "You're going back to Seattle with us when we go, aren't you?"

"I guess I am."

"Goodness, it's hot. Why is it so hot? I didn't eat anything on the train except toast and tea. I couldn't. The dining car was filthy. I feel faint. I hope somebody at your house knows how to cook. All Mother knows how to make decently is beef stew and egg custard. We have a cook at home. Who does the cooking at your house, Ellen Grae?"

"Oh, I do some and Jeff does some. We eat a lot of delicatessen stuff."

"What are we going to have for dinner tonight?"

"For supper, you mean? I thought we'd have some chicken and dumplings. I called up Mrs. McGruder—she's the lady I stay with when I'm not living with either Jeff or Grace—and asked her how to do it. Her dumplings are just grand. She makes them Southern style. I hope mine will turn out as well as hers."

Laura pressed a handkerchief to her damp forehead. "I don't especially care for chicken. Couldn't we have steak instead?"

I leaned out of the car window and saw Jeff staggering out of the station house. Under each arm he had two brown, oblong suitcases and both of his hands were full. Aunt Eleanor trotted beside him; her hands were empty and she was laughing. Jeff was trying to share whatever it was she was so merry over but the suitcases kept shifting and sliding and his face showed strain.

Jeff is gallant. He'd have died of a coronary thrombosis attack rather than ask Aunt Eleanor to take one of the cases.

On the way home we stopped at a meat market and bought five steaks—the extra one was for Grover in case he decided to show up for the evening meal but he didn't that first night.

Aunt Eleanor was polite about the salad I made to go with the steaks and the way I set the table but she said she could see that I needed a little instruction in hostessing. "The dinner fork always goes to the left of the plate," she said. "And since we're having salad we'll each need a salad fork. You see? Like this."

"Yes, ma'am. I understand. Thank you for telling me."

"Also one provides saucers for coffee cups and a bread and butter knife for each diner." She looked at me. "Do you feel all right, dear?"

"Oh, yes, ma'am. I feel just fine, thank you."

Aunt Eleanor's smile is bonny, like Jeff's. She gives it to people wholly, the same way he does when he likes them. Smiling at me she glided around the table, rearranging the salad plates, the silver, the napkins, and the water glasses but all the time she was doing it I could see that her mind was more on me than the table setting. I could see her making one mental note of everything I did wrong and another one to remind herself to correct it. The air in the house was so hot it almost hurt to breathe it but there was a chill, northwesterly wind blowing in the pockets of my brain.

The steaks didn't turn out too well because we have an old stove and its broiler is recalcitrant but everybody was valiant about it. Afterward I washed the dishes which took me an hour because there were so many of them and then Laura showed me how to roll up my new curls on big mesh rollers for the night. "To look well groomed is something you have to work on every day," she said. "A permanent is just the basis for beautiful hair."

I made the mistake of admiring her long, silken eyelashes and she said they cost her six dollars and were made out of real human hair. She took them off and showed them to me and gave me an extra pair she had. They made my eyes water and itch but she wouldn't take them back. She said I'd get used to them.

Before I go to bed all I do is brush my teeth and put on pajamas which only takes me about two minutes. But it took Laura an hour to get ready. First she cleaned her face with cream and then went over it with cotton which had been soaked in ice water. Then she creamed it again, then she oiled her knees and heels and elbows, rolled her hair up and tied a scarf around it, brushed her teeth for three minutes, and exercised for five before an open window. She said she had a horror of getting thick through the waist.

I didn't sleep much that night. Jeff and Aunt Eleanor, carrying on a murmuring, low conversation in the living room, kept me awake until after twelve o'clock and then I had a nightmare. In it I was on a train which was hurtling down some tracks and Grover, with a dreadful grief in his face was running along beside it pleading with me to jump off and come back to Thicket. I tried to, but Aunt Eleanor screamed for the conductor and he came with a big, steel chain and wrapped it around me and locked it and with a cruel smile ordered me not to move out of my seat. We finally reached our destination and I was led off the train, still imprisoned

in the chain and everybody stared and leered and
threw snowballs at me. It was so cold that all the
blood in me congealed and I fainted but no one came
to my rescue. A girl with huge feet and white, dis-
passionate eyes came up and stuck an icicle into me
and said, "Why, it's Ellen Grae from Thicket but she's
quite dead. Ha, ha, ha, ha, ha, ha!" And the snow
fell on me and covered me and I *was* dead.

The dream woke me and then I was unable to go
back to sleep. I got up and knelt at the window and
looked at the dark sky and listened to the night-bird
notes drifting in from the field. From Aunt Eleanor's
room, which had the door open to allow cross-cur-
rent ventilation, came a soft snore.

In the middle of the night thoughts run freely because there is nothing to distract.

Dawn came but nobody except me got up. I
couldn't think of anything to do at that hour that
wouldn't disturb everybody else so I took a walk
down the road to the egg lady's place. Her husband
said she was in the hospital with two new babies and,
while he counted out three dozen eggs, told me all
about them. He was pretty excited and worried.

We didn't do much that day except go to town to
buy me some new shoes and dresses and a raincoat.
For me it was an ordeal but Aunt Eleanor seemed to
enjoy herself. In the dress shop the saleslady had a
long, snooty look for my underneath pants which I
admit were a little on the tacky side—loosely baggy
with the lace which had once been crisply attached
to the leg holes torn and limply hanging. But Aunt
Eleanor just smiled a cool, svelte smile and said, "My
niece is from another planet. Her people have a glorious disregard for what covers their little bottoms.
Could we see the little checked suit again, please? I
might have changed my mind about it."

Like Jeff, Aunt Eleanor is hybrid.

After the dresses and raincoat we went to another
shop where they sold Exquisite Lingerie For M'Lady,
and Aunt Eleanor went hog wild. I told her I didn't

care one twit for all that frivolity but she bought me a pile of it anyway, even some blue lace stockings and a wide mesh belt to hold them up with. I didn't ask how. The heat and all that pawing and decision-making enervated me.

Finally we got through and Jeff and Laura met us at a restaurant for lunch and then we went home. Jeff worked on a landscape painting, Laura watched television and Aunt Eleanor set up the ironing board in Jeff's bedroom and went through his wardrobe, looking for anything that needed to be mended or pressed. I sneaked out the back way and went over to the McGruders.

Mr. McGruder, who is an amateur numismatist, was working on his coin collection. He showed me two Maria Theresa dollars he'd just acquired. "Hear you're going out to Seattle," he said.

"Yes, sir, I reckon I am."

He turned his large, friendly eyes on me. "By the time you get back we probably won't know you."

"Oh, sure, you will. I might change a little inwardly but outwardly I'm not going to. You'll know me when I get back, all right."

Mr. McGruder fingered the two Maria Theresa dollars in their cellophane envelopes. Something in his face shifted back and forth. "Like to hear from you once in a while," he said.

"Yes, sir, I'll be sure and write to you. Is it all right if I use your encyclopedias for a few minutes? I want to look up some stuff about hair."

"Hair?"

"I want to find out some things about it. Where's Mrs. McGruder?"

"In the kitchen. Ellen Grae?"

"Sir?"

Mr. McGruder, with a wrenched look, leaned and took my hand and pressed one of the Maria Theresa dollars into the palm of it. "To remember me by," he said.

More than a friend is this dear and generous man.

The McGruders' high-beamed kitchen is a meeting place. It is the heart of their home, always steady and good humored. Mrs. McGruder is usually in it as she was that day. Elbow deep in flour she said she was sick and tired of the air-blown bread sold in stores and had decided to try making her own.

"Grace and Jeff and I made some one time," I said. "That's when all three of us lived together. Jeff kneaded it until it cracked but it still didn't do any good. It still didn't come out right."

Interest sparkled in Mrs. McGruder's face. "Oh? What happened?"

"It exploded. We were making tomato juice at the same time and forgot about the bread and when we finally remembered it and opened the oven—"

"Excuse me," said Mrs. McGruder. "But before you go on with the bread what did you say you were making besides it?"

"Tomato juice. Somebody gave Jeff some tomato plants and to make them grow faster Jeff bought a chemistry set and mixed up a lot of chemicals and every morning and every night we soused them good with it. Pretty soon we had tomatoes as big as canta loupes and we couldn't eat them all so we decided to make juice out of them. So the day we decided to make the bread that's what we were doing—making tomato juice. They squeeze pretty easy, easier than oranges. That's before Jeff had sold even one painting and we didn't have much money. But anyway, after we got all the tomatoes squeezed, we happened to remember the bread which Jeff had put in the oven to let rise. Jeff jumped over to the oven and opened the door and a great, big, white balloon popped out of it. I poked my finger in it and it exploded. Whooooosh!"

Mrs. McGruder laughed. "Oh, Ellen Grae."

"Ma'am?"

"Nothing. I was going to say that without you there's going to be quite a hole in my life but I don't need to say it, do I? We both know that already, don't we?"

The McGruder kitchen is a rallying place but I left it very much un-rallied.

On the way home I met Grover who was on his way to our house to eat supper with us, he said. "You look different," he observed. "What's wrong with your eyes?"

"Nothing. I'm wearing false eyelashes, that's all. Where were you all day?"

"My uncle and I went fishin'," he answered and leaned forward for a closer examination of the lashes. "Wimmin," he said, mourning their dishonesty. "They'll do anything for looks. Where'd you get 'em?"

"Laura gave them to me. Grover, I'm worried sick."

Grover scratched his stomach and breathed. "I am, too, Ellen Grae, but I can't think of anything to do to change things. Just keep hopin' is all I can tell you. Maybe it'll work out so's you won't have to go."

On his deathbed Grover will probably say, "Maybe it'll work out." I never get any help from him in a real crisis.

Supper was dull. Listless beef stew and egg custard and phlegmatic conversation. Jeff said he hoped it would rain soon. Laura said she thought she'd get to work the next day on getting a light suntan to take back to Seattle with her. Aunt Eleanor said she thought she'd phone Mrs. McGruder and find out who the best hairdresser in Thicket was and she was sorry about the beef stew but she simply wasn't accustomed to cooking for a lot of people.

Grover sighed.

To liven things up I studied over a piece of interesting truth I knew about, decided that none of it was my imagination, and took the plunge. "The egg man's wife had Siamese twins today. Joined at the stomach. They're going to operate on them so they won't have to go around hooked up together all their lives."

Jeff glanced at Aunt Eleanor, took a careful bite of his custard and laid his spoon on his plate. He said, "Siamese twins, eh? *That* ought to put Thicket on the map. How did you find out about this before the newspapers, Ellen Grae?"

"I was down there this morning before any of the rest of you got up. We needed some eggs and I needed something to do. The egg man doesn't want any publicity, that's why it wasn't in the afternoon paper. He trusts me is the only reason he told me."

"Oh, we won't tell anybody about it," Jeff said and excused himself and went to his den and we heard him telephoning and then, after five minutes or so, came back to the table for another cup of coffee. "The egg man's wife had Siamese twins today," he said to Aunt Eleanor. "Joined at the stomach. They're going to operate on them to see if they can't be separated. He doesn't want any publicity so don't let this go any further."

This piece of news, even though it was the truth, livened up the evening—gave us something to talk about besides Seattle and hair and clothes and what we should have to eat the next day. Grover went home and got a book out of his uncle's library and came back with it and he and Jeff pored over pictures of Siamese twins for an hour. Grover direly predicted that the twins would die because there was only one stomach between them but Jeff heartily observed that in his opinion the twins had a good chance of survival—that the doctors wouldn't attempt it if they didn't think so. Aunt Eleanor said it was a tragic thing and made her ill just to think about it and didn't we want to watch the movie on Channel Four? Laura helped me clean up the supper mess. Then she took another bath and gave herself a pedicure.

When Grover got ready to go home I walked with him as far as the road. "Seattle's great clam country," he said. "I been readin' about it. They got a clam grows out there that gets to weigh twelve pounds sometimes. It's the largest burrowing clam in the whole world. You know what its name is?"

"No, Grover."

"Gooeyduck. That's how they pronounce it. Gooeyduck. It sounds like a bird but it isn't. It's a clam. You spell it G E O D U C K. A long time ago the people out there used to call them hyas squish-squish. A man named Mr. John Gowey—he was the mayor of Olympia, Washington—went hunting for ducks one day but didn't get any and came home with some of these clams instead. They named it Gowey Duck and then later started calling it gooey-duck. They dig 'em with big clam shovels out there. Ellen Grae, you listening to me?"

"Yes, Grover. Listen, how would you like to take Aunt Eleanor and Laura and me for a little boat ride tomorrow?"

"A boat ride? You mean fishin'?"

"No, I don't mean fishing. I mean just a little boat ride down the river and back."

Grover scratched his stomach and shuffled his feet. "Well, I wouldn't mind, but what for?"

"I want Aunt Eleanor to see that I can be as much of a lady as Laura even in primitive surroundings. When she sees that I can be she'll tell Jeff and maybe he'll—"

"What kind of surroundings?"

"Primitive, Grover. Primitive. That means uncivilized. I swear if I ever get through with this ordeal I'm going to work on your vocabulary. I swear it's terrible."

"I'll meet you at the boat at nine o'clock tomorrow morning," Grover said. "You watch yourself when you go back to the house, Ellen Grae. Maybe you'd better go straight to bed so you won't have to talk to anybody about anything. But if you *do* have to stay up and talk, say just as little as you can. Remember, I won't be there to stop you if you start one of your stories."

He needn't have fretted. The rest of the evening was lackluster.

First we talked about hair. There was an old movie on television and it was in color and the heroine's hair was a beautiful, flaming red and Laura was moved to wonder aloud if it was natural.

Jeff, who was trying to read the evening paper, said it looked natural to him.

Aunt Eleanor, with a lapful of Jeff's shirts, all of them needing buttons, took a stitch and asked what difference did it make whether it was natural or not.

Laura, with a bored look, said, "It doesn't make any. I was just wondering, that's all. Assunta, that's our maid out in Seattle, dyes hers and it's the same color. She denies doing it but sometimes you can see the gray at the roots. I *know* she dyes it."

Aunt Eleanor took two more rapid stitches. "Laura, Assunta is *not* our maid. She is a member of our family. And she does *not* dye her hair. She might put a little tint on it once in a while but she doesn't dye it. If you knew anything at all about it you'd know there's a big difference."

I hauled out my newly acquired knowledge. "Yes, there certainly is. I never used to have any interest in hair but lately I have a lot because Jeff wants me to be feminine. I want to be that way, too, so I looked up some things about hair. And you know when you're doing that how you just keep on reading and reading even when you've already found out what you wanted to find out? Well, anyway, I came to hair dye and found out it's based on paraphenylenediamine. This ingredient penetrates the hair shaft partly and forms an insoluble brown dye when it's oxidized by air and peroxide. Hair tint you can wash out because it doesn't do anything to the hair shaft except coat the surface."

Jeff's smile, over the top of his paper, was bloodless and there was pain in his eyes.

After hair I directed everybody's attention to another safe subject—food. "If everybody's agreeable we
could have shrimp tomorrow night for dinner. It
comes in fresh twice a week at the market downtown. I'd like you and Laura to taste some of our
good Florida shrimp while you're here, Aunt Eleanor.
They're good almost any way you fix them. Grace
likes hers curried best but my favorite is Creole style.
That's the way they fix them in New Orleans a lot.
One time before Grace and Jeff got their divorce
they took me to New Orleans with them and we ate
shrimp cooked every way there was: Shrimp a la
King, a la Newburg, curried, fried in batter, minced
up Louisiana style, cooked in a cheese souffle, put in
aspic, chow mein shrimp, and baked in a pie. I like
Creole best. To make it you boil your shrimp about
ten minutes—not longer because if you do they'll
turn tough—then you clean them and then you add
them to Creole sauce. To make the sauce you use
butter and onion and mushrooms and some minced
ham and flour. I like shrimp Creole. Of course, curried
shrimp is good, too. To make curried shrimp you use
chopped onion, butter, curry powder, pimiento, some
peas, some rice, shrimp, milk, salt, and water. First
you fry the onions but don't let them brown. Then
you take the flour and the curry powder and salt and
mix all of these ingredients together. Then you add
some boiling water, after which you add the milk and
the shrimp. Then you put in the rice and some pimiento. If that sounds good to you could I make you
some tomorrow? If you don't think you'd like that
I could always make shrimp a la Newburg. The only
trouble with shrimp a la Newburg is that the recipe
calls for sherry and brandy and we don't have either
one. I could make a shrimp loaf if you think you'd
like that. You use fresh mushrooms in shrimp loaf,
and egg yolks. It's very good."

Jeff, who is seldom fervent about anything, fer-
vently said, "Lord help us," and got up and took his
paper to another room to finish reading it.

"I hate last minute invitations," I said to Aunt Eleanor, "and I know you must also, but Grover and I would like to take you and Laura for a little boat ride tomorrow morning. We want you to see how beautiful and peaceful the country around here is."

Aunt Eleanor said she and Laura would be happy to go for a boat ride with Grover and me. She suggested bed so that we'd be rested for the outing.

There ensued another restless night. I dreamed about Seattle again and it was so real that I had to get up and search for a blanket to put over me but even then warmth didn't come.

Chapter 4

THE NEXT DAY was at first reluctant, pallid, and foggy. But then the haze lifted and the sun turned a fierce, energetic red. The temperature began a hot, stifling ascent.

While I was packing the lunch for our boat trip Jeff appeared to drink his morning glass of milk. He observed that I looked like a girl should look, all neatly brushed and tied and buttoned. He wanted to know where Grover and I were going to take Laura and Aunt Eleanor.

"Oh, just on a little boat ride down the river," I told him. "I want them to see how pretty it is around here. I want to see how pretty it is again myself. It'll probably be the last time I see it for a long time. Maybe I'll never see it again. Did you read about that man who fell out of the door of the plane he was on, Jeff? He plunged eighteen thousand feet to his death, poor thing."

Jeff finished his milk and wiped his mouth on a napkin. "Well, maybe there's a lesson to be learned from his demise. Maybe it'll teach other travelers to stay away from open airplane doors. Personally, his fate rather taxes my imagination since doors on planes don't open as easily as house doors, contrary to what you might think. Still, if you say it happened, I believe you."

"Oh, it happened, Jeff. The paper said he was a drug fiend. Probably he was crazed from it. A lot of strange people ride around on planes, blowing them up and doing other crazy things. I read about this other man —he was a Communist—who made the pilot turn the plane around and fly down to a cannibal island. Of course all the passengers had to go along, too. Wouldn't that be a terrible thing, Jeff?"

"Terrible," agreed Jeff, preparing to make coffee. He said, "You should take your camera along today, Ellen Grae. Maybe you'll see your otter and can get a picture of him this time."

"Otter? What otter?"

"The one you and Grover found sick in the swamp last year and gave an appendectomy to."

"An appendectomy. Isn't it funny I don't remember that?"

Jeff plugged the percolator into a wall socket and sat down and waited for the coffee to perk. "You found him out in the swamp beside a stump, sicker than a dog. His appendix had ruptured and peritonitis had set in. Grover had his first-aid kit in the boat and you rushed back for that and then back to the otter. You made a mask out of some gauze and dripped ether on it to anesthetize the little animal and then you and Grover operated. In the middle of this proceeding Grover got sick and had to lie down so you carried on by yourself. The operation was a success and now, the way I hear it, the otter is as happy as a lark, recognizable from other otters because of his scar. Remember it now?"

Through the thick, irritating fringe of my false eyelashes I looked at my father. "That never really happened, Jeff. It was just one of my stories."

Jeff unplugged the percolator which had done its job and poured himself a cup of coffee. There was an unleashed sigh in his eyes.

The day began to have a rancid feel to it.

Jeff didn't say anything more and neither did I except to ask him if he didn't want to go along boating with us. He said no, that he had too much to do and buried himself in the morning paper.

Eventually Aunt Eleanor and Laura appeared, prettily dressed in white skirts and red peasant blouses and wide sun hats. After they had drunk orange juice and eaten two doughnuts apiece we gathered up the lunch basket, the Thermos jug filled with ice water, a clean sheet for us to spread on the boat seat so we wouldn't get ourselves dirty, soap and towels so that we could wash ourselves, if necessary, and set out.

The path that led us through the field and down to the river was crackling dry. A friendly snake with hooded eyes and an Adam's apple gently flicked his cold-blooded tail as we went past him.

Grover, looking lusty and nautical in spanking white trousers and shirt and a new gold-braided captain's cap, was sitting in the bow of the boat waiting for us. A marsh raccoon peered down at us from an overhanging bough, his mouth full of breakfast.

So courtly in manner that I almost didn't recognize him, Grover helped Aunt Eleanor and Laura into the boat and spread the sheet out for them to sit on. I climbed in by myself, arranged all the stuff we had brought along so it wouldn't slide around, and sat down, too.

Grover looked around at me. "Well, if we're goin' anyplace you'll have to cast us off, Ellen Grae."

There wasn't any help for it. I had to remove my

shoes and socks and climb back out of the boat and shove us off. It slid away from me so quick that I almost didn't make it back in, but Grover didn't even notice.

Aunt Eleanor did though. She said, "My."

We moved out to the middle of the stream with just Grover paddling. I dangled my feet over the side of the boat to get the mud off and put my shoes and socks back on. Beneath us the water smoothly rippled. Overhead the sun broke through the overhanging trees and something on the bank of the river angrily chattered and there was an explosion of wings. The flag, attached to the stern of the boat, fluttered in the soft breeze.

"This is nice," said Laura.

Grover's chest swelled. "I'll take you downstream where there's some scenery like you never saw before. I brought some bait along—maybe you'd like to try and catch a fish. There's some real big ones in this ol' river."

Aunt Eleanor said, "Oh, no, let's not do any fishing, Grover. Let's just enjoy the boat ride."

"Oh, no, you got to catch a fish," said Grover with his best fisherman's smile. "It's lots of fun. Ellen Grae will bait your hook for you; you don't have to worry about that part of it." He turned and looked at me. "Hey. I *thought* this thing was pullin' a little hard. If we're gonna go anyplace you'll have to help me row, Ellen Grae."

So I had to help him row which is an exercise I usually enjoy but didn't that day. My muscles bulged like a boy's with every dip and pull of my oar and I couldn't keep my skirt dainty like Laura's and after a few minutes I started to sweat in a very unladylike way.

Grover had forgotten the purpose of our journey. He catcalled to a two-foot-long alligator basking himself in a puddle of sunlight on the right bank of the river, hooted at birds, and plied his oar with such energy that I had trouble keeping up with him.

When we went around the bend in the river he turned his head around and shot me a reproaching look and said, "Hey, what's the matter with you this morning, Ellen Grae? Why you layin' down on the job?"

Specifically, fishing had not been on the agenda but Grover, playing the host, insisted that we do some. We reached a spot in the stream which was dappled with shade and he called, "Rest your oar, Ellen Grae! This is a good spot!" And rested his own oar and scooted forward and leaned for a look down into the polished water. Then he stood up and pushed his captain's cap to the back of his head and said, "Yep, this here's a good spot to fish in. Break out the bait, Ellen Grae."

Protests would have been useless; they would have only caused Grover to jaw. So I secured my oar and opened the bait bucket. Aunt Eleanor and Laura recoiled at the sight of the pink worms wriggling around in their bed of moist, black earth but Grover, all puffed up, said, "Aren't they nice and fat? Bait up a hook, Ellen Grae, and show your aunt and Laura how to catch a fish."

There was no sense pretending squeamishness or ignorance. Grover was in one of his exuberant moods and would only have laughed and made the situation worse. So I rigged up a fishing pole with some good, stout line and a good, strong hook, selected a worm, fitted it to the hook, stood up and inched over to the side of the boat and lowered the weighted line into the water. The end of it had barely sunk beneath the water's surface when a fish struck. I gave the pole an expert flick and my victim, a small-mouthed bass, leaped to the surface, twisting and turning and spraying droplets of water.

Aunt Eleanor gasped and Laura clapped both hands over her mouth.

"Haul him in!" screamed Grover. "Don't let him get away! Haul him in!"

The bass, solidly hooked, put up a vigorous battle

but I finally got him to the side of the boat and Grover yelled for Laura to reach under the seat for the landing net and between us we flipped him into it.

Laura wiped her forehead with a tissue and weakly smiled at me.

Aunt Eleanor said, "My."

"For Ellen Grae that was easy," Grover crowed. "She can do almost anything I can. But come on, let's go downstream a ways. Maybe we'll see somethin' interesting."

By the time we put into shore thirty minutes later the day had turned light and sweet. A white-bellied heron met us but after one disinterested look stalked off through the wiry grass. We got out of the boat and Grover and I pulled it up on the bank and then we looked around. There wasn't really much of anything to see but Grover, glowing with importance and enthusiasm, kept hopping around, hollering for everybody to come look at this and that. A banner of silver-green Spanish moss floating from a limb of a tree that was at least fifteen feet high caught Aunt Eleanor's eye. Grover cried, "Oh, you want that to take back to Seattle with you? Wait a minute—I'll get it for you." He backed off and got a running start and then charged forward and leaped up on the defenseless tree and shinnied up it, snatched the moss from the limb, and hurled it down.

"My," said Aunt Eleanor.

Grinning, Grover peered down at her. "You want some more? You want a piece to take back to one of your friends?"

Aunt Eleanor picked up the length of moss and spread it with her fingers until it became a lacy scarf. "Yes," she said. "I'd like several more pieces of this to take back with me. People out in Washington don't know what it is. But be careful, Grover. Oh, my, if you were to fall and hurt yourself."

"Don't worry," sang Grover. "I'm always careful." Overly confident, he threw down another big hunk of moss, started to descend, somehow caught the back of his belt on a protruding limb, couldn't let go to work himself free, and I had to go up and rescue him.

Aunt Eleanor was moved to gently remark that she had never seen a girl climb a tree with such agility.

Grover tried to enhance my reputation. He said, "Well, Ellen Grae's not like most girls."

I got him to one side and said, "Grover, *please* don't remind Aunt Eleanor that I'm not like most girls. I realize you think that's a compliment and maybe it is but please don't point it out to her. If you feel you've got to say something about me, tell her what a little lady you think I am."

Grover sucked his cheeks and looked sorry. During lunch which we ate in the boat because of the danger of crawling insects on land he slyly tried to rectify things by saying to Aunt Eleanor that he hadn't meant to say that I wasn't like *most* girls. He said, "What I meant to say was that Ellen Grae isn't like *some* girls."

The day was a fiasco. On the way home Laura fell overboard and if it hadn't been for me might have drowned.

The return trip started out well with the river softly surging but then suddenly, the water turned hostile. At first it was just a stealthy movement, as if some great serpent beneath us had awakened to become resentfully aware of our presence. But then as we glided into a shadowed widening the water heaved and breathed and gasped and took possession of us. It lifted the boat and rocked it from side to side and then there was a lurch and then a plunge and Laura was thrown into the water.

Aunt Eleanor screamed.

Grover, for some reason, let go of his oar. I heard it clunk against the side of the boat and saw it go bobbing off with the current. With an alarmed look,

Grover jumped to his feet, hesitated for just a second, then dove after it.

"To heck with the oar!" I cried. "Hell's afire!"

But Grover went after the oar.

It didn't look to me like Laura was in any critical trouble. Her head was above water and she was making some grim efforts to keep it that way but Aunt Eleanor, wildly white, was hopping up and down and yelling to me that Laura couldn't swim.

I jumped up and kicked off my shoes. A flashing parade of objections coursed through the calm part of my mind. It would ruin my hair and my dress. I am not a dainty swimmer; my strokes are too strong for daintiness. Rescuing people is a boy's job—not a girl's. But there wasn't anybody else to do it so I dove into the warm, chocolate-colored water, swam out to Laura, got a rescue hold on her, and towed her back to the boat. I almost got drowned myself while doing it because she weighs more than I do and Aunt Eleanor's wails were distracting.

Grover, back on board himself, hefted her up and into the boat but left me to my own resources. "What happened?" he asked. "Did we hit a log or somethin'?"

In a box of emergency supplies which Grover always keeps in the boat there was an old pair of his pants and an old shirt. Aunt Eleanor shook out the sheet we had brought along and held it up and made Laura get behind it and change her wet girl's clothes into Grover's dry ones and we resumed our homeward journey.

Safely back on solid earth Aunt Eleanor said she was grateful to me for saving Laura but that, in her opinion, the river was no place for a girl. She said she couldn't understand Jeff, letting me roar around the country the way I did with Grover.

Grover, with an alien hauteur, said he thought Laura should learn how to swim. "I knew how to swim when I was four," he said and helped himself to a banana from the fruit bowl and went home.

Jeff and I had a private porch talk. He commended me for my bravery but said he was compelled to agree with Aunt Eleanor. That the river was no place for a girl and that the way I roared around the country with Grover was a positive disgrace to the name of Derryberry and my sex. He said that if his mind and Grace's hadn't been entirely made up before about sending me to Seattle that now it thoroughly was.

He said, "Today I bumped into Sheriff Fudge downtown and he asked me how my son was. I told him I didn't have a son and he laughed. Needless to say, I was not amused."

There is a loneliness that comes from a wasted day.

Jeff's distress was contagious. During the night it metastasized—transferred itself from his being to mine. I developed nervous bumps and raven eye rings.

Chapter 5

BUT WE DERRYBERRYS have sinewy genes.

I asked Jeff the next morning if he believed in metamorphosis and it startled him so that he put a red splotch where an orange one belonged. After he had cleaned it off with his palette knife he said, "Now what was your question, Ellen Grae?"

"I asked you if you believed in metamorphosis."

"Metamorphosis? Certainly. Every organism exhibits change throughout its life."

"I'm not talking about organisms, Jeff. I'm talking about humans."

With a sweep of his brush Jeff created a flaming

sun on his canvas. "Well, humans are organisms. What are you eating, Ellen Grae?"

"An egg sandwich. Eggs are part of the metamorphosis I'm talking about that's taking place in me. I'm looking for some big, new values, Jeff."

Jeff subdued his sun, and his basalt landscape, darkly gleaming, took on a retiring look. He cleaned his brushes and laid them on a stand to dry. A glow came into his mercury-colored eyes. Extending hope, he said, "That's fine, Ellen Grae. That's just fine."

The day was humble and expeditious. Jeff and Aunt Eleanor went to Sarasota to deliver some paintings—she just for the ride. About nine o'clock Grover appeared. "Going to take Laura down to the river and give her a swimming lesson," he announced with a vigorous look. "But it's top secret so don't tell anybody if they get back before we do."

I watched them go, Grover in the lead carrying an inner tube to assist in the swimming lesson, a hoe to kill snakes with should any poisonous ones cross their path, a first-aid kit to doctor insect bites and scratches, a rolled-up towel, and a jug filled with ice cubes and water.

With just me in it the house, which Jeff had rented for his summer in Thicket, was destitute. Unlike houses that families live in year after year this one had not mellowed. It had an air of neutrality and impermanence.

I went outside and looked at the day but its appearance made no impression. I thought about Seattle, so close to the shivering border of Canada and what it would be like to live there. I raked my brain trying to think of other ways to keep Jeff and Grace from sending me there but nothing came. I was as clean as soap and water could make me, hair curled and brushed, sweet, with a ribbon in it, teeth gleaming, nails shaped and scrubbed. I had stopped telling lies. My room was straight, clothes all neat on hangers, the floor swept, the bed made, nothing under it except a few books I kept there for night reading when sleep wouldn't come.

I had done all that I could do. Now my fate was in the hands of Destiny.

It came back from the river with Laura and Grover about eleven o'clock. Laura's elegant white swimsuit was mudstreaked, she was sunburned, her curls were sodden strings, her makeup was smeared. But she said that she had had a marvelous time learning how to do the butterfly stroke and the Australian crawl.

Grover, with his brown hair plastered to his head and his face all gritty with sand, went to the refrigerator and helped himself to a hard-boiled egg, a stalk of unwashed celery, and a handful of grapes. He stuffed a little of each into his mouth and pumped his jaws. "I'm clean tuckered," he declared. "I got to go home and rest a while."

Laura peeled her false eyelashes from her eyelids and laid them on the table. "They're all right for dresswear parties," she said, "but in the water they make my eyes itch." With both hands she lifted her hair from the back of her neck and made an untidy ball of it. "It's such a nuisance," she said. "I wanted to learn how to dive but I couldn't see a thing with all this hair hanging in my eyes."

Grover's red and white grin was enigmatic. He said, "Yeah. For divin' you got to have short hair. Long hair gets in the way."

Destiny was at work.

In the afternoon before Aunt Eleanor and Jeff got home Laura took a pair of scissors and whacked at her hair until it was shorter than mine. She said she only had intended to take about an inch off, but once she got started she couldn't stop. "I gouged it," she said, showing me a denuded spot on the back of her head. "And then it just kept getting worse and worse. What are you making?"

"Shrimp Creole. You want to help?"

"I don't think so. I'm worried about what Mother will say about my hair. I honestly don't know what came over me while I was cutting it. I only intended to take off about an inch."

I opened a can of mushrooms. "Well, if your hair's like mine it'll grow back."

With her upper teeth Laura gnawed her clean, lower lip. "Grover's lots of fun. He's cute too. All the boys I know back in Seattle are so dull. All they do is stand around with their mouths open. You'd think they were born that way. I just mortally despise boys who are so dumb they don't know enough to close their mouths. They're so . . . wet."

I said, "Grover's got a nice, tight mouth. He never lets his hang open."

Laura tugged at a lock of her chopped hair, lifted her bare, dusty right foot, and rubbed her sunburned left instep with it. There was a new kind of smile on her lips and a new kind of expression in her eyes. "Grover showed me his worm bed," she said with a calm and secret smile.

Something strange had happened. Something mighty strange.

Aunt Eleanor and Jeff came home about five o'clock. Aunt Eleanor sniffed the shrimp Creole and said that she just knew it would be delicious. She inspected the table and only moved one fork.

Jeff, with the kind of look he wears when he has a headache, said that coming home always restored him.

Aunt Eleanor said she thought she'd freshen up a bit before dinner and went to her room. There was a little period of silence throughout the house and then I heard Aunt Eleanor call to Jeff and he went down the hall to her room and stayed a minute or two and then he came back to the kitchen, all bristles. He said, "All right, Ellen Grae."

"Sir?"

"Whose idea was the barbering job?"

"You mean Laura's hair? Jeff, I didn't have a thing to do with it and that's the truth. I didn't even know about it until it was done. Didn't Laura tell you?"

"Yes," replied Jeff. "She told me but are you sure you didn't influence her just a little bit?"

"Jeff, I swear I didn't. A very strange thing has happened, Jeff. If you'll give me a minute I'd like to tell you about it."

Jeff's smile was thin, bordered with frosty skepticism, but he pulled a chair out from the table, placed his hands on his knees and leaned forward in an attitude of attention. "All right, you've got a minute. Let's hear about this strange thing that's happened."

I walked over and stood in front of him and looked deep into his silver eyes. "Well, Jeff, this is going to sound a little weird. I hardly know how to say it. But do you know what's happened?"

"No, but I'm trying to find out."

"Let me tell you what's happened. Laura and I have had a personality transference."

"A personality transference," echoed Jeff with a tragic, half-smile.

"Yes, sir. Laura has become me and I have become Laura. Just our personalities, I mean. I don't know how it happened or why but it's happened. Have you ever heard of such a thing? I only noticed it about an hour ago. When she came out here with her hair all whacked up that's when I noticed it. You notice it when she comes to the table, Jeff, and see what you think. Maybe it's some kind of defense mechanism at work."

Jeff put a hand to the back of his neck and pressed. "Some kind of defense mechanism."

"Yes, sir. Oh, I don't mean in *me*. I don't feel defensive toward Laura and her personality. I am very receptive to Laura's kind of person. I *want* to be like her. She's so sweet and pretty and has such nice manners. But this transference of personalities has taken place and—"

"Ellen Grae."

"Sir?"

"Your aunt and I bought luggage for you while we were in Sarasota."

"Oh."

"And we have a few sensible things to talk about between now and the time you leave."

"Yes, sir."

Jeff's hand moved from the back of his neck and went to an uncertain resting place in his lap. Over the planes of his face there spilled a silent, fragile tide. "We haven't talked at all about the new life you're going to find out there. You haven't asked me one question about it."

I looked at him straight, straighter than I had ever looked at anybody and I tried to think of a question to ask about the new life I was going to find out in Seattle but all the words in me were hiding.

So we didn't talk about it then.

About eight o'clock Grace telephoned to say that she couldn't get away from her job in Miami long enough to come up and see me before I went to Seattle. When she said good-bye to me it was like doom.

Grover came over and when I told him the news he put his hand inside his shirt and scratched with such passion that I could hear the skin coming off. He said, "I never thought it would happen Ellen Grae I sure didn't I sure thought between us we could get you out of it Seattle Oh Lordy."

Before I went to bed Jeff and I had our talk about the new life I was going to find in Seattle.

My faith in myself and my abilities was shaken as never before.

Came THE TIME. It was like a funeral. The train pulled into the station and two men got off and Aunt Eleanor and Laura and I got on. Standing on the platform Mrs. McGruder pressed her handkerchief to her mouth and Mr. McGruder feebly waved his. Jeff's face, floating above his body, had an inflexible smile stamped on it. Grover's was red and stiff as a board.

. I pressed my own face against the cold pane of the window and stared out at them.

There was a jerk and the wheels beneath us began to turn.

Aunt Eleanor in the aisle seat beside me said, "You'd better sit down now, Ellen Grae. We're moving."

I sat down and put my nose against the thick glass of the window and held it there until it was numb. Until all of Thicket was left behind.

We Derryberrys do not cry. Not even at funerals. Well, not much, anyway.

Chapter 6

BETWEEN THICKET AND TAMPA there lies a long, curved span of land that few northerners have ever laid eyes on for the superhighways leading in and out of the state have not yet encroached here. This is Cracker country, as mean and stingy a piece as you would ever want to see. The shacks that squat in random array along the railroad bed are patched with Orange Crush and Coca Cola signs. The old faces that look out of their doors as the trains thunder past are tiredly patient. The young ones are quick and curious. Most of the yards are broom-swept and have flower beds bordered with upturned glass bottles. All of the yards have black, iron wash pots but no clotheslines. The laundry is spread on bushes to dry.

In winter, from the train windows, you can look out and see this forgotten wilderness, all silvered with frost and the smoke from the chimneys rising straight

up, pearl plumes in the still, cold air. In the summer-
time it steams.

"I don't believe I'd care to live back in here," commented Aunt Eleanor. "How about you, Ellen Grae?"

"Oh, I don't reckon I'd mind it. I wouldn't mind
being born and living and dying all in one place.
Probably the people who live back in here aren't
afraid of anything."

Aunt Eleanor took my bare, chilled hand in one of
her warm, gloved ones. "No, probably they aren't.
But consider fear for a minute. Fear is one of the big,
human experiences. What if you didn't know what it
was?"

"If I didn't know what fear was then I'd be ignorant. Unless they're dumbbells everybody knows what
fear is."

Aunt Eleanor patted my hand and smiled her
queenly smile and beckoned to the porter, who was
in the rear of our car talking with Laura, and ordered
us each a cup of coffee. I told her I wasn't allowed to
drink it but she just said, "Oh?"

The airport at Tampa was windy and international.
A Latin-American family guarded their island of hand
luggage. A priest read a Mexican newspaper and
watched the clock. A lady in a lovely yellow sari said
good-bye to a man with a sculptured white beard. He
kissed her hand.

Up close planes look different than they do in the
sky.

Laura said that to look down from heights gave her
vertigo so I got to sit by the window. The stewardess showed me how to fasten my seat belt, there
was a lot of fidgeting and settling all around, then
there was a long rush forward during which the man
across the aisle kept his eyes closed and then we went
straight up into the blue atmosphere. I looked down
and saw the earth beneath us, a sheet of brown and
green-checked gingham, strangely silent and motionless.

In the seat ahead of Laura and me Aunt Eleanor

took a book from her bag and opened it to the first page. The stewardess came with a tray of fresh fruit and Laura selected a banana because they don't drip and I took a peach.

The man across the aisle swallowed a pill and went to sleep. Laura asked me what was wrong with my peach and before I thought I told her the truth—that it tasted like salt.

Time was temporarily embalmed.

We had lunch. The man across the aisle woke up but didn't eat any. After it we lowered and I looked down and saw that the tapestry of the land had undergone a dramatic change. Broad, open plains rolled in all directions. Rivers glinted in the sun and orderly green and yellow meadows appeared anchored to the earth.

"Wheat or soybeans," informed the stewardess, looking down with me. "We're over Illinois."

We came into Chicago, landed and stayed there for an hour. It went fast.

When we got back on the plane to resume our journey Laura asked me how I liked Chicago and I told her that the city might be all right, though I hadn't seen any of it, but that I thought the people were a little on the desperate side. "All that pushing and shoving and washing in the rest room. I never saw so many people in such a hurry to get washed. I only counted one person who wasn't. It wore me out."

Laura opened her purse and took out an emery board. "I'm going to do my nails. Want to do yours?"

"No, thanks. They haven't had a chance to grow much since the last time. You know something? I think people in transit are pretty terrible, the way they push and shove and snap and won't help anybody. That poor lady in the rest room back there was in an awful fix but nobody even offered to help. We had to empty three wastebaskets before we found her watch."

Laura applied the emery board to her thumbnail.

"I wish I had some colored polish. You don't have any, do you?"

"No. I don't have any kind. That was the most beautiful watch I have ever seen. All encrusted with diamonds and pearls and sapphires. She said it cost her husband twelve hundred dollars and he'd kill her if she lost it. The safety catch on it had broken. I found it in the third wastebasket. She was terribly grateful. She said if I ever got out to Hollywood, California, for me to be sure and look her up. You know something, Laura?"

"No," Laura replied. "I don't know anything."

"That couldn't have happened in Thicket," I said.

From Chicago to Montana I slept. When I woke up and looked out and down I saw a column of purple mountain peaks, draped in snow, stretching as far as the eye could see.

Over Idaho there was a rainbow.

Eastern Washington looked thirsty. Aunt Eleanor said that it was. But after we had passed over the Cascade Range, rich dairyland and a moist, verdant spread of forest-studded land laced with grass appeared. And after that there was the skirt of Seattle, "Queen City of the Northwest."

"We're home," said Aunt Eleanor.

We had a long, undulating ride.

"Seattle is built on a series of hills," said Aunt Eleanor.

The streets were clean and the buildings did not lean against each other as they do in Thicket but stood erect and independent. In the sky above the city there hung a gigantic etching of a frosted mountain. I thought I could make out a man with a knapsack on his back crawling up its craggy side, it looked so close, but Aunt Eleanor said that it was miles away. "That's Mount Rainier," she said.

The back of the taxi driver's neck was clean. He had a prosperous smile.

Aunt Eleanor's house sat on a thick, green rug with a rose-bush border. A row of lilac trees shaded the entrance. It had a door with a knob in its center which opened without anyone touching it and an inscrutable, beige face, studded with a pair of washed-blue eyes, looked out. The name which belonged to it, said Aunt Eleanor, was Assunta.

Usually when I meet a stranger I can tell in about five minutes what kind of person he or she is and then I can mold my personality to his so that both of us can be comfortable. But Assunta was like porcelain. She led me to the room I was to occupy and, thinking to please her, I told her how pleasant and pretty it was but she just grunted. "Just do me a favor and hang up your own clothes," she said. "And when you get up in the mornings open all the windows and air your bed. Sleep's got a funny smell to it and people leave it behind in their beds."

I said, "Yes, they certainly do. Sometimes my bed at home smells so bad it almost stifles me when I'm trying to sleep. I always air it out real good though when I get up in the mornings. Usually I hang my sheets out on the line so the wind can blow out the smell."

Assunta's look was dry and unresponsive. "It won't be necessary for you to do that here. If you'll unlock these suitcases I'll help you put your things away."

"Oh, I can do that. I don't need any help. I didn't bring very much because I'm not going to be here very long. Is this the closet? Oh, yes, I see that it is. My, what a big one."

"I like things put away neat and straight," said Assunta. "So if you'll just unlock these suitcases for me we can stop wasting time."

I unlocked the suitcases. Some of what was inside one of them was private but Assunta scrutinized everything. "What's this?" she asked, holding up a jar.

"That? Oh, that's just a little memento a friend of mine gave me."

"A memento of what?"

"Of the swamp near Thicket, Florida, where I live."

"It looks like dirt."

"Yes, ma'am, that's what it is. It's dirt from the swamp near where I live in Florida. I didn't especially want to bring it but Grover—that's my friend— brought it down to the train just as we were getting on it and I didn't know what else to do with it so I stuck it in my suitcase."

Assunta walked across and set the jar of dirt on the dresser and returned to the suitcase. A wrinkled garment with a vermilion paint splotch on its left breast was held up for inspection. "What's this?"

"It's a shirt."

"Yours?"

"It is now. It used to be my father's. I wear it when I go fishing."

"I see. These pants go with it?"

"Yes, ma'am."

"They're kind of big for you, aren't they?"

"Not when I get the belt that goes with them on."

"This belt?"

"Yes, ma'am."

"Kind of big for you, isn't it? Looks to me like it'd go around you twice."

"Yes, ma'am, it does, but doubled like that it holds my pants up better."

Assunta refolded the shirt and the pants, made a tidy coil of the belt, walked to the bureau and laid all three items in a drawer. Returning to the suitcase she said, "We should come to some dresses pretty soon. If we don't I'll begin to have my doubts about you. Oh, here's one. This looks like Sunday. Is it?"

"I don't know. I haven't worn it yet. In Florida I don't go to church much except when I live with the McGruders."

Assunta made the muscles in her mouth work, drawing the lips together. "Oh, yes, the McGruders. Your aunt wrote and told me about them. They make you go to church when you live with them?"

"Oh, they don't *make* me. They don't *make* me do anything."

Some more of Assunta's lips disappeared into her mouth. "So I understand."

"Ma'am?"

"Nothing."

"I just go to church with them out of respect. Their church, I mean. They're Methodists and I'm a Pantheist."

Assunta shook out the froth of lime-colored silk. "That sounds interesting. I don't know as I've ever met a Pantheist before."

"Pantheists don't worship in churches. We can worship under a tree if we want to and it doesn't have to be on Sunday. We don't have preachers either. It's a beautiful religion. We don't have to go to prayer meetings or church suppers or get dressed up or anything."

Assunta carried the dress to the closet, slipped it on a hanger, returned to the first suitcase which was now empty, closed it and started on the other one. But after four pairs of socks and two slips she said, "I think I'll let you finish this. Use the rack in the closet for your shoes. Don't put them on the floor."

"Yes, ma'am."

The shadows in Assunta's sterilized eyes were cool. "I hope you'll be happy here."

"Thank you, ma'am. I hope I will be, too. I think I will be because it's my nature to be happy wherever I am. Of course I don't intend to be here very long so it won't matter much if I'm not."

Assunta had a bloodless smile.

After the suitcases Aunt Eleanor and Laura showed me the rest of the house. It had a lot of velvet chairs and many gilt-framed mirrors. The back door opened out on to a flat deck with steps which led down to the lawn. The rim of this emerald-colored strip dipped into Lake Washington where small pleasure boats bobbed like sitting ducks. There was a weather-gray pier and we walked down to it and looked out across the expanse of water.

Laura and Aunt Eleanor were both beside me and

their faces and attitudes were friendly but in this vast, alien place I felt my personality shrink and my equilibrium waver. I felt that I could have walked away from myself and looked back and not recognized what was left standing there.

"Isn't it beautiful?" asked Aunt Eleanor and Laura.

"Yes, beautiful," I answered, hating it.

The sun's warmth was frugal. We walked back up on the lawn and I knelt and touched a patch of it. It was moist and cold.

One by one the boats on the lake disappeared and the sky lowered and darkened.

"I think we're going to have a little squall," said Aunt Eleanor and we went inside.

For supper we had clam chowder which reminded me of Grover's telling me about gooeyducks so I couldn't eat much.

The squall passed over us and sped westward, spinning a gray, hazy veil as it went.

Until ten o'clock, someone with a dull bronze head played a harp in a lighted room in the house next door.

"That's Smith Smith The Seventh," said Laura. "He's practicing for a recital he's going to be in."

I wasn't really interested but to make conversation I asked how old he was and Laura said he was twelve and had a sister by the name of Victoria who was eleven.

Smith Smith The Seventh's celestial music followed me into my room and went to bed with me. It made me think of wings and time and distance and for a long time sleep didn't come. Forgetting where I was I got up and looked under the bed for my Thicket antidote but there wasn't anything there. No books, nothing, not even dust.

And again, as on the pier that afternoon, I felt this awful shrinking inside myself which was like a physical sickness, so pressing and acute that it brought tears to my eyes and I had to go to the bathroom and vomit.

Chapter 7

ON MY SECOND DAY in Seattle there was an earthquake.

It came without a sound. At first there was just the light fixture on the ceiling lazily swinging back and forth. Lying in my bed, only half awake, its languid motion was fascinatingly remote. What a strange house this was—how different from Florida houses where light fixtures do not swing unless they're touched.

Today, now that my mind was rested and clear, I was going to figure out a way to get myself back to Thicket.

The motion of the frosted globe wasn't balanced. Whoever or whatever was making it swing wasn't paying attention.

The windows framed squares of pale sunshine and the air was still and cool. In Thicket, because of the time difference between Washington and Florida, it would be about eleven o'clock.

The pendulum on the ceiling picked up a little speed and the word poltergeist came slipping into my mind. Against my cheek the pillow was smoothly comfortable; it smelled clean. I closed my eyes but immediately opened them again because there was something under my bed thumping it and making it bounce.

"Hell's afire," I said and sat up and tried to get out of it but it slid first backward and then forward and then sideways with such vigor that the headboard was knocked catawampous and one of the legs buckled.

113

"Hey, listen!" I hollered. "Hey, what do you think you're doing? Stop it now! Stop, you hear? Listen! Look what you're—what do you think you're—hey! Oh, my gosh!"

All of a sudden there was big motion and noise everywhere. The windows started to chatter, making an awful racket. The hangers in the closet rattled. The door flew open and two boxes fell out. A vase on the dresser toppled. A chair rushed across the room and crashed into the wall. A crack appeared in the wall above the dresser and spewed bits of plaster.

I struggled to conquer at least the bed. "Hell's afire! What the heck . . . hey, look what a mess you're making in here! Stop it now! Stop that, you hear?"

The chair had gone berserk. It danced away from the wall and ran over to the dresser and whacked it. Mortally wounded, the mirror attached to its top, fell out of its frame.

Disgusted with our one-sided battle, the bed punched me, violently discharging me, and I staggered away from it to the door. One of its hinges had been wrenched loose but I got it open and looked out.

The door to Laura's room, parallel with mine, was jerked open. Laura appeared in its frame.

"For God's sake!" I hollered. "What's going on anyway? There's something crazy in this house! Maybe a murderer! I'm going to call the police or somebody! Where's the phone?"

Laura was green to the gills. "Earthquake!" she screamed. "We're having an earthquake! Stand in your doorway! It's the safest place!"

Aunt Eleanor with her nightgown swirling around her came sprinting out of her room just as another shudder walloped the house but when she saw Laura and me standing in our doorways returned to her own. "Don't move!" she shrieked. "This is a bad one! Don't move!"

Something within the bathroom crashed to the tile floor. A toothbrush came sailing out and landed in the corridor between Laura and me. It wasn't mine.

I thought about God and Grover and Grace and Jeff and Mr. and Mrs. McGruder.

Another convulsion passed under and through the house but then abruptly the quaking and all of its accompanying noise stopped.

Laura, the color of a ripe avocado, looked at me and swallowed. "Maybe it's over," she whispered.

I listened to the silence. "Yeah," I said. "Maybe it isn't, too. An earthquake, for God's sake. Why didn't somebody tell me?"

Some tentative minutes passed and then Aunt Eleanor said, "I think it's over. I think it's safe for us to move about now."

In the street in front of the house there was a fissure an inch wide. We were without electric power until noon. Half of Aunt Eleanor's rooftop chimney was gone. Laura and I went outside to pick up the strewn bricks and then examined the street fissure, a disquieting sight.

"Hell's afire," I said. "If it had kept on widening it could have swallowed us up whole, house and all."

Laura touched her thatched hair. "I've been in lots of earthquakes. We have them here a lot but I never thought about . . . well, it *could* happen, couldn't it?"

"Of course! If the edge of the earth broke off or split open wide enough this whole town could fall in or this whole state! Or this whole country! I know a lot about earthquakes even though our specialty in Florida is hurricanes, not earthquakes. They're caused from earth faults. See, inside the earth there's a lot of strain going on all the time and when it gets to be too much then comes an earthquake. You're sitting on a great big fault right here. I read someplace that there's a huge one out here. At any minute it could decide to open up and swallow this whole town or this whole state or this whole country! One time in California they had an earthquake and it killed about a thousand people. The fires it caused were terrible. One old grandfather who was just standing there holding his baby—"

"*We're* sitting on a great big one right now," said Laura with a gently reminding look.

"Yes. We. I meant to say 'we' because I'm here now. But anyway, this old grandfather—"

"Here comes Smith Smith The Seventh and his sister," said Laura. "He's the one who knows about earthquakes."

Smith Smith The Seventh and his sister Victoria got down on their knees to examine the fissure. "Nice," said Smith Smith with a pleased, scientific look. "I wonder what this quake will measure on the Richter scale."

"Probably over seven," said Victoria and the orange polka dots on her white cheeks and nose quivered.

Laura introduced me to the Smiths.

"How do you do?" they asked, as one.

I said, "Well, I think I'm all right now but about this earthquake. What's a Richter scale?"

The Smiths had olive green eyes with queer, khaki-colored spots in them and soft, tired voices. Smith Smith The Seventh said, "The Richter scale is a logarithmic scale devised by Dr. Charles Richter and Dr. Beno Gutenberg of the California Institute of Technology which provides a quick and easy means to classify earthquakes as to size."

"We know a lot about earthquakes," apologized Victoria, "because we used to live in Japan. As you know, they have some pretty large ones over there."

"In Florida we have hurricanes," I said. "I don't know what they use to classify them as to size but some of them are real buggers. The last one I was in was about . . . well, I reckon I was about nine. Usually when we know one is on its way we boil up a lot of water and cook up a lot of food and board up all the windows but this one came tearing in from the Gulf one morning without giving us time to do anything. It turned black as night, just all in a second, and the river, which isn't far from where I live, boiled up yellow and then this terrible wind came, so loud that you couldn't hear yourself think. I ran out to get some clothes off the line—I knew they'd be whipped to pieces if I didn't—and while I was doing that this tree that was a hundred years old was ripped up from the ground, roots and all, and hurtled into the air and all of the birds that had been roosting in it fell out of it with broken necks. The wind had done that. There isn't any fury on earth like the fury of a hurricane."

"The Beaufort scale is used to designate the force of hurricane winds," said Smith Smith The Seventh with a brooding look.

"I beg your pardon?"

"The Beaufort scale, named after Admiral Sir Francis Beaufort who drew it up in 1806. The weather people use other wind instruments, too, but I especially remember reading about the Beaufort scale."

"We know a lot about hurricanes," apologized Victoria, "because we used to live in Key West."

In Smith Smith The Seventh and Victoria I recognized my peers.

Chapter 8

SEATTLE IS A CITY of many occupations and the people who live in it so industriously pursue life that they haven't got time to sit around bellyaching over things like earthquake damage and near brushes with death. The excitement the earthquake caused died down in about two days.

Laura and I went to town just to look. We saw a machine that belched hot doughnuts—one every second; tried on hats in a department store but didn't buy any; swapped stares with a cigar-store Indian who stood in the window of a curiosity shop. The man who was dusting the Indian looked up at us and grinned and we went inside and looked at an old ship's bell and a Chinese beheading sword.

We took a ferryboat ride over to an island and afterward stood on a corner and watched a parade and ate a foot long hot dog. A high-stepping man in the parade winked at us. Then we had to go home because we were out of money.

On another day Aunt Eleanor took Laura and me to a park named Volunteer and in it there was a building which housed the Seattle Art Museum. We looked at the sculptured Ming-dynasty camels on its steps and inside went around gawking at the permanent collection of Chinese jade which was centuries old and at the rich display of contemporary art. One poignant one reminded me of Jeff but we Derryberrys are all self-contained so I didn't say anything. Outside we looked at Puget Sound and the haughty, frozen rampart of the Olympic Mountains, which rose beyond this body of water.

We went to a Japanese restaurant and sat on the floor and dangled our legs in a hole and ate *sukiyaki*, a kind of stew made of meat, sliced bamboo shoots, fish paste, snow peas, and Chinese cabbage. Before I found out it was just plain raw fish camouflaged in soy sauce and green horse-radish I ate a dainty helping of *sashimi*, too.

Because of the *sashimi* relations between Assunta and me improved.

"Did you know what it was when you ordered it?" she asked with a shine in her antiseptic eyes.

"No."

"Then why'd you order it?"

"Oh, I figured as long as I'm here I might as well try a little of everything. Want me to iron some for you?"

Assunta shook out a dampened tablecloth and

spread it across the ironing board. "I don't think so. I'll stop in a minute and fix you some breakfast."

"Oh, I've already had it, thank you. I've already had my breakfast and got the paper read and hung my sheets out on the line. You sure you don't want me to iron? I do it for Mrs. McGruder sometimes when I'm home. I could have all that done for you in about twenty minutes."

The iron in Assunta's hand hissed steam. She set it on the tablecloth and made a wide swathe. "You couldn't do all *this* ironing in twenty minutes. Look at it—there must be a hundred pieces. I don't know where it all comes from."

"At home I never iron tablecloths; they take too much time. You know what I do with them? I hang them out on the line and hose them real good. Then when they're dry all I do is fold them. That's one shortcut I figured out. Another one is shirts and blouses. When it's cool weather most people wear sweaters and jackets so what's the sense in ironing *all* of a shirt or blouse? I don't. I just iron a little bit of the front and the collar."

Assunta's iron slowed. She turned her head and eyed the basket of pieces to be ironed. "Yeah? And you never get any complaints, huh?"

"Oh, once in a while I get one. Rosemary—that's the girl I have to room with when I live with the Mc-Gruders—gripes some. She never gets out of bed until the last minute. She goes off to school in her sleep so she never knows what she's got on until about the third period. She gripes some when I iron her stuff but people get over things. I don't consider ironed clothes one of life's big, important values, do you?"

"No," replied Assunta with a comradely look, "I don't."

"What *do* you consider some of life's big, important values?"

Assunta finished the first tablecloth, folded it, and started on another. "What do I consider some of life's big, important values? Well, money comes to my mind first."

"Money isn't a value. It's a necessity."

"Ha," said Assunta. "You'd think it was a value if you didn't have any. If you had to sleep under a tree instead of in a bed. Or if you had to eat out of a garbage can instead of off a plate."

"I wouldn't mind sleeping under a tree. It wouldn't bother me a bit. Assunta, do you like it here? In Seattle, I mean?"

"Sure," replied Assunta. "If I didn't I wouldn't stay."

"Where would you go if you didn't like it here?"

"Oh, I don't know. I'd figure out someplace where I thought it was better."

"How would you get there?"

"How would I get there? Well, if I had the money I'd get on a train or a bus. If I didn't have, I'd hitchhike. Hitchhiking isn't a bad way to travel. Of course you can't always pick your own company when you choose that way to get from one place to another. It can be risky. Not all ladies driving down the road in white Cadillacs are ladies; some of them just look like they are. Some of them would just as soon chop your head off and feed it to the first wild animal that came along as look at you. In fact, they'd rather."

A mental picture of a wild, vicious animal, hungrily standing by the road, waiting for my bloody head to be tossed out to him so that he could devour it, jumped into my mind.

"Besides," said Assunta, "hitchhiking is against the law in most states now. You can get yourself locked up for it. So if I were you I wouldn't even think about it. If I were you I'd stay here and try to make the best of things. It isn't so bad. You're just a little homesick right now; you'll get over it. Do me a favor, will you? Go and see if your aunt and Laura are awake. If they aren't, don't wake them. Let them sleep till noon if they want. When they do, it just makes my job that much easier."

Aunt Eleanor and Laura were sound asleep, both of them gently snoring.

Pleased with this little morsel of serendipity Assunta put her ironing away and said she thought she'd mop and wax the kitchen floor. She invited me to go and find entertainment elsewhere.

I went outside and walked down, through the wet grass, to the pier and looked at Lake Washington. Its shredded waves were the color of steel; its distant shoreline lay masked in thick fog. The air was eerily silent and coldly moist. I thought about Thicket and a sense of loss swept over me, a sickening feeling of nothingness. If I, just at this moment, moved my feet forward and stepped off into the water and let it close over me, who would notice? Not Assunta, so absorbed in her housecleaning. Not Aunt Eleanor nor Laura, so sleep-obliterated in their rooms. Nobody would notice until it was too late, until my body, sagging with water, rose from its cold grave to horrify them and make them sorry. Oh, how sorry they'd be! Jeff and Grace would come and stand in the hushed chapel of the funeral home and they'd look down at my still, lifeless form and their grief would be so terrible they wouldn't even be able to cry. The minister would be there and he'd hand them each a tapered candle and they'd light these and hold them in their shaking hands and someone would come with a wreath of yellow roses and then the lid of my coffin would be closed and the bells would toll their anguished message.

How lovely it would be, how satisfying.

But wait. *I* wouldn't be there to see it. I'd be dead and people who are dead can't see anything. They aren't spectators, they're victims. I *might* be able to look down and view what was happening but then again I might *not*. And what if I wasn't? If I wasn't, my sacrifice would all have been for nothing. Besides who wanted to die? Not I. No, sir, not I. I had a problem to lick but what of it? I could do it. Something would come to me. It always did.

Hoping for inspiration I went back up to the house and tried to have another conversation with Assunta but the wax smell in the kitchen was so overpowering that I couldn't.

From the living-room window I watched Victoria and Smith Smith The Seventh, who were down on their pier, grapple with something that appeared to be a large, white butterfly. Aunt Eleanor came out of her room and looked and said that it wasn't though. "It's a new sail for their catboat," she said. "Are you all dressed, Ellen Grae?"

"Oh, yes, ma'am, I certainly am. I've been up since about six. I'm ready for anything you are. What are we going to do today?"

The pink feathers on the collar of Aunt Eleanor's dressing gown waved as she moved away from the window. "We're going to have luncheon with Admiral Ford and his wife. Don't you remember I told you we were last night? I think you'd better change into something a little nicer. Come on, I'll help you choose."

Something nicer was a navy blue dress with a white sailor collar, a slip, pants with pink rosettes, the blue lace stockings we had bought in Thicket, the wide mesh belt to hold them up with, shoes with bows on their toes, a white hat borrowed from Laura and a pair of white gloves, also borrowed from Laura.

I was instructed by Aunt Eleanor to take a bath, scent myself with some body cologne, strap the belt around my middle, put the pants over it, put the slip on over those two pieces and then call for Laura's assistance.

With part of this done I stood in the middle of the room and looked at myself in the mirror. I was acquainted with slips and pants but the belt, so stiff and taut, so *binding* was another story. Its dangling straps, two short ones in front and two longer ones in back, made me think of the suspenders that Jeff sometimes wore under his suit coats.

"I don't see why I have to wear this contraption," I said to Laura. "What do you call it anyway?"

Laura took the blue lace hose from their box and handed them to me. "It's a garter belt. It's to hold these up. Put them on."

"You mean on top of everything else I'm supposed to wear *those?* What for?"

Laura sat down on the edge of my bed. "These are stockings, Ellen Grae. They're to cover up your legs and make them look pretty."

"My legs don't need to be covered up. They don't need to look pretty. Listen, Laura, I'm already five pounds overweight with all this other stuff on. So why don't we just skip the stockings? It's a little bit chilly out today. My legs are blue enough without them. Look at them if you don't believe it. See the veins? How blue they are?"

"Ellen Grae."

"What, Laura?"

"They won't kill you. It's just a pair of stockings. They only weigh about two ounces."

"I know that. Don't you think I know that? It's not the weight that gripes me. It isn't honest, that's what gripes me. My legs aren't blue, they're brown so why should I try to make people think that they just naturally grew blue? Have you ever seen anybody with naturally blue legs? Look at this leg now. You know what it makes me think of, blue like this? A raw turkey."

Laura took a roll of mints from the pocket of her robe, peeled off two, stuffed them into her mouth and sucked. "As soon as you get the other one on we'll start hooking you up," she said. "You want a mint?"

"No, thanks, I just want to—listen, Laura, this is utter. I swear it is. You'd think they'd at least have sense enough to make these things fit. I feel baggy. Look at how much is left over. Get me a pair of scissors, will you? I'm going to cut some of it off."

Supremely calm, Laura leaned and took the top of

the right-leg stocking in her fingers, drew one of the dangling straps down to meet it, tucked the rubber eye that was attached to the end of it, snapped the metal hook that was also attached to it, and one-fourth of the job was done.

My cologne, activated by nerves, rose to my nostrils in a hot, overpowering wave.

Laura sucked her mints, said, "There," and moved around to work on the back but in the middle of this proceeding the rear strap broke.

"It's broken clean through," murmured Laura. "Right in the middle. Must've been defective. Now it's nothing to get nervous about, Ellen Grae. Hold still a minute. I think I can tie this up, the two broken ends together, I mean. See, like this. It makes a little bulge but I don't think it'll show through your dress. Oops, wait a minute. Let me make another knot. I don't think this first one's going to hold. It's slipping. I swear, this sure *is* a contraption, isn't it? Funny I never noticed that before. I've been wearing garter belts for two years now and I just never noticed it."

Laura *can* be a compatriot. She knows how to impress people and make them like her, too. Both Admiral Ford and Mrs. Ford told me how fond they were of Laura.

"She's such a little lady," said Mrs. Ford, looking at me through her pince-nez. "The Admiral and I want to take her to Washington, D.C. with us the next time we go. I have a nephew in the Pentagon and he has a son about Laura's age. I want them to meet. What part of Florida did you say you were from, dear?"

"Thicket, ma'am. That's near Tampa."

"Oh, yes, Tampa. Where they make the cigars. I really don't like Florida. It's so hot and flat and there are so many bugs. Go and talk to the Admiral, dear," she said. "I just want a few minutes alone with your aunt and Laura and then we'll have lunch."

The Admiral, who was not a cheery man, took me from room to room and showed me his souvenirs.

Going up the stairs to look at two flintlock pistols lying in a velvet-lined case he told me what good friends he and Laura were and what high hopes he and Mrs. Ford had for her future. He stroked his mournful mustache and caressed the guns and said, "I knew her father. A fine man. A really fine man. Very courageous. Very courageous. Loved adventure. Once he persuaded me to fly down to Brazil with him. Not for any special reason—he just wanted to see how it would feel to live in the jungle for a few days."

I looked into the Admiral's big, umber face and warmed to him. "Did you find out?"

The Admiral's eyes filled with chilly pride. "Indeed we did. Indeed we did. We hired a guide and went way back into the jungle and lived with a tribe of Indians for a week. Some of them had never laid eyes on a white man before but we didn't have one bit of trouble. Not one bit. They gave us one of their huts to sleep in. We shared their food and water. They showed us how to hunt and fish Indian-style. For ten days we were completely removed from civilization."

"Sounds to me like you had a fine time," I said.

The Admiral rationed a skimpy smile. "Oh, not all of it was fun. There were parts of it that were very dangerous. Very dangerous. Some of their tribal customs, for instance, were closely guarded secrets; we were warned not to try and spy on them. They might have killed us if we had. Once, during one of their ritualistic celebrations one of the old chiefs went quite mad. Laura's father and I were sitting in our hut, waiting it out, and we heard the commotion but even at a time like that we didn't dare look out. We might have been able to help but we didn't dare to even offer."

"What happened to the old chief? What did they do to him?"

The Admiral replaced the guns and closed the case. "I don't know. We never saw him again. I hope that they merely put him away but I suspect that they might have killed him."

I said, "I had an experience like that one time. One time Grover and I—Grover is my friend—were out in the swamp just looking around for anything interesting that might turn up and we came to this pit and this poor homicidal maniac that had escaped from the mental hospital at Chattahoochee rose right up on us and nearly scared us to death. Grover wanted to run and I reckon I did, too, a little bit because she was gnashing her teeth and screaming at us in the unknown tongue and we could hear the dogs that were out looking for the poor old thing baying and howling and barking and we could hear the men in the sheriff's posse getting—"

"She was screaming at you in what?"

"The unknown tongue. A lot of people from the south can speak it. It isn't hard. It goes something like this: *Mork anta blanstirgal aba sentaracolum! Grastarbuna lorka serat frizamcrampul!* That's the unknown tongue. But anyway, there we are out there standing by this pit and Sarah—we found out that her name was Sarah—was pulling her hair and gnashing her teeth and screaming at us in the unknown tongue and the sheriff's posse was getting closer and closer all the time and it was very scary, with them shooting off their guns and yelling to each other. Yes, sir, it was very scary, I can tell you. But I said to Grover, 'Listen, Grover, we've got to help her.' Well, Grover didn't want to help her, not in the way *I* wanted to help her. You know how *he* wanted to help her? He wanted to give her a Rorschach test, if you can imagine such a thing. With Mercurochrome because we didn't have any ink. All we had was our first-aid kit with Mercurochrome in it."

The Admiral's eyes were glacial. He covered them with his lids.

"There wasn't anything pretty about it; it was very bad, I can tell you. But anyway, after I talked some sense into Grover and talked to Sarah until she became passive he took hold of one of her arms and I took hold of the other and we ran her back to the boat. I gave her a tranquilizing pill to calm her down more than she already was and then we took her back into town and turned her over to Sheriff Irby Fudge. All he did was put her in his car and take her back to Chattahoochee. Poor old thing. She cried when I left her. She said she loved me and would never forget me."

Admiral Ford's tongue was a bright, shiny pink. He wet his shriveled lips with it. "Is that all of your story?"

"Yes, sir, that's all of it."

"Then we'd better go back downstairs," said the Admiral and smiled his thin, pale smile. "Lunch will be ready."

Mrs. Ford's food was the best I had ever, eaten. I complimented her on her cooking and Laura was quick to side with me but our praise didn't please either Mrs. Ford or the Admiral. They were lovely people but I wasn't attuned to them nor they to me.

I wasn't attuned to Seattle either, though it was nice enough, and I racked my brain until it ached, trying to think of a way to get myself back to where I belonged but nothing came to me until I went sailing with Victoria and Smith Smith The Seventh.

Chapter 9

IT WAS TWO DAYS LATER and again Assunta was ironing and again Laura and Aunt Eleanor were sleeping late and again I was wandering around looking for something to occupy my mind. Neatly arranged on the coffee table so that the colorful, glossy covers would show, Aunt Eleanor's magazines offered advice to brides and entrapped wives but nothing to people like me. I read a story about a girl with satin hair and a man with tragic eyes who fell in love in an elevator. Riding up and down in it every chance they got, both of them were feverish and wretched for a month but neither of them did anything about their plight until the last paragraph and then all they did was say hello.

The mailman delivered a letter from Jeff and one from Grover. Jeff's said that it was unusually hot in Thicket and that everybody had asked about me, even Irby Fudge, the sheriff. Grover's said that he wasn't doing much fishing. For once, he said, he'd be glad when school started.

I went outside and looked at the day. The air was like crystal but there was an energetic wind over the lake, whipping its waves into a feathery, white froth. In the misty distance a powered pleasure boat created a mischievous wake. Its red pennant was saucy.

Standing on the Smith pier were Smith Smith The Seventh and Victoria. Tied to it, straining at its lines, was their catboat.

"We're going sailing," said Victoria. "If you'd like to come along there's plenty of room."

I took a good look at the boat which looked nautical enough but a little on the skitterish side.

"We're Navy," apologized Victoria. "So you don't need to be afraid. Smith and I know a lot about boats. Our father taught us."

I said, "Oh, I'm not afraid of boats. This looks like a fine one. Where are the oars?"

With a ravaged expression Smith Smith The Seventh said, "Ellen Grae, this is a *sailboat*. You *sail* it; you don't *row* it. We have oars; they're stored there in the cuddy cabin but we only use them in case of emergencies." He went past me and climbed down into the cockpit of the boat.

Victoria and I followed and Smith Smith directed me where to sit "because balance on a sailboat is important." "Also," he said, "it's important that I tell you about the boom."

"The boom," I said. "I don't think Grover has one of those on his . . . what's the boom?"

"This," explained Smith Smith, laying his hand on a heavy, wooden pole to which one end of the sail was attached, "is the boom. On a sailboat it's something to watch out for. If we're running before the wind and we jibe it'll swing across the boat to the opposite side and if you aren't watching out for it you'll get a nasty crack on the head."

"One time it happened to me," said Victoria, her orange polka dots agleam. "But it wasn't Smith's fault. He's a good skipper."

Smith Smith The Seventh sniffed the wind and flexed his gangly legs. "Just watch out for it. Especially watch out for it when I give the command to come about."

Victoria looked at her brother and me and smiled.

Smith Smith The Seventh inflated his gaunt chest. "All right, let's cast off the bow line."

There was a flurry of practiced activity. Victoria cast off the bow line, took the stops off the sail, and raised it. Smith Smith let the nose of the boat swing around. The sail filled up with wind and Smith Smith cast off the stern line.

Under easy sail, without any laboring or straining, we moved out into the open water. The power boat, which had moved up closer to the shore, slid by, careful not to create a nuisance with its wake. Smith Smith and Victoria saluted its captain.

A duck with a green velvet head paddled by and Victoria took a slice of dried bread from her pocket, pinched off a piece, and threw it to him.

Another boat, with its sails spread like a lovely moth, appeared on the horizon.

The wind was at our backs and it freshened suddenly and Smith Smith The Seventh at the tiller said, "Reef the sail a little, Victoria."

Victoria got up and reefed the sail a little.

With my palm I examined my forehead. Beneath the skin the bone felt hard and strong.

The palette of the sky slowly took on color. In a beautiful attitude the sailboat on the horizon sped before the wind.

"Prepare to come about!" suddenly bawled Smith Smith and I remembered the boom and ducked my head and felt it pass safely over and we changed course and sailed off in the opposite direction.

The duck with the velvet head, or one just like him, paddled up again, this time bringing one of his friends, quacked for another handout, and Victoria gave it to him.

Spray glittered as it blew aft. Despite the sun's valiant efforts it was cold. I thought about Thicket and again this strange, displaced sense came over me. Somehow, I thought, I've got to get back to where I belong. Even if it kills me I've got to do it.

Now when I stop and think back on what happened next I can't separate how much of it was accident and how much of it was on the inspiration of the moment. Were I pressed, though, I would have to say that most of it was inspiration-of-the-moment.

"Why don't we," I said to Smith Smith, "change our course again? This one's getting kind of monotonous, isn't it?"

The khaki spots in Smith Smith's eyes jumped to life. "Yes," he agreed, as if discovering it for himself. "Yes, it is."

"Let's turn around again," I suggested. "That was fun."

"Yes, it was," agreed Victoria and smiled at me.

My forehead bone started to queerly jerk but I ignored it.

"Stand by to come about!" bawled Smith Smith The Seventh.

Victoria stood by to come about.

I didn't.

I saw the boom, at least three inches in diameter, swing toward me.

Victoria screamed. "Ellen Grae! Duck! Duck!"

I didn't duck.

KAWHOOMP. *Mark anta blanstirgal aba sentaracolum! Grastarbuna lorka serat frizamcrampul!*

Chapter 10

THERE FOLLOWED A TWO-DAY STAY in a hospital during which the bump on my forehead got X-rayed twice. The skin above my eyes and all around them turned a deep, pulsing purple.

My nurse's name was Lana. She was German.

In the bed next to mine there was a fat lady who was supposed to get thin but couldn't because her relatives sneaked food in to her. I counted ten of them—each brought her something.

Aunt Eleanor came and sat beside my bed for thirty minutes. Our conversation was desultory:

"How do you feel?"

"All right, except my head aches a little. Do Jeff and Grace know I'm in here?"

"Yes, they know. Tell me something, Ellen Grae. When you saw that boom on the boat coming toward you why didn't you duck?"

"I don't know, Aunt Eleanor. I just . . . well, I just felt kind of queer sitting there watching it come toward me. Mesmerized, you might say. Well, I know this sounds a little strange, doesn't it?"

"Very strange," replied Aunt Eleanor with a forthright, searching look. "Very strange. Did you tell the doctor about this?"

"No, ma'am. I didn't think he'd want to know about that part. Are you sure Grace and Jeff know I'm in here all banged up like this?"

Aunt Eleanor drew on her white gloves. "Yes, they know. I phoned them."

The fat lady in the bed next to mine took a chocolate cream from a box beneath her pillow, popped it into her mouth, chewed and swallowed it, and said that she thought she might be getting ready to have another of her palpitations.

Aunt Eleanor conveyed get-well wishes from Laura, Assunta, Smith Smith The Seventh, and Victoria and left.

The doctor came in and looked at the bump on my head again. He said he wished he had a head as hard as mine.

For lunch we had broiled fish and boiled spinach. The fat lady said that for her such a poor excuse for a meal was impossible and took a hunk of liverwurst, two hunks of rye bread, a slab of chocolate cake, and two bananas from her purse and dined behind the screen that hid the sink from the rest of the room. When she emerged from it and huffed over to her bed and sat down she said she thought she could feel a strengthening in her blood.

I saw a dazed man go wobbling past our door and then a minute later saw Lana go streaking after him.

"Probably he escaped from surgery," commented the fat lady. "In a place like this it's hard to know who your friends are."

Hospitals are such dolorous, harried places.

In the early afternoon the fat lady had her palpitation but Lana didn't come until it was almost over. It was just a little one.

About four o'clock the phone she and I shared rang and it was Jeff. He said, "How do you feel?"

"Not too good. Not too bad. My eyes are black clear down to my chin."

"Tell me about the accident," he said.

"The accident. Yes, sir. Well, sir, Smith Smith The Seventh and Victoria and I were out sailing around on the lake. Smith Smith said for us to stand by to come about—that means for everybody to watch out for the boom because in a sailboat when you jibe, the boom swings across the boat and if you aren't watching you could get a nasty crack on the head. Which is exactly what happened to me. Smith Smith said for everybody to stand by to come about and Victoria did but I didn't and that's all."

Across the distance that separated us Jeff's voice came floating back. "Why didn't you?"

"Why didn't I stand by to come about? Well, sir, to tell you the truth I . . . well, Jeff, I was just sitting there and I was thinking about Thicket . . . to tell you the truth I didn't have my mind on what was going on . . . I was feeling kind of queer, watching the water and the boom, mesmerized by it all you might say. . . . And I was just sitting there thinking about Thicket and all of its dear people and how nice and warm it must be back there . . . here it's so cold and damp . . . and Smith Smith . . . well, I asked him why we didn't turn around and go back in the other direction and he said that was a good idea and said for everybody to stand by to come about and I looked at the boom . . . I remember I did that . . . but then . . . then I didn't do anything about it. I didn't duck. I just let it . . . well, Jeff . . . listen, are you still there?"

"Yes, Ellen Grae, I'm still here. Do you have a cold?"

"No, sir, I don't have a cold."

"You're not crying, are you?"

"No, sir, I'm not crying. I don't have anything to cry about. I'm a very lucky person just to be alive. I very nearly got killed. I can tell you when I saw that boom coming toward me it nearly scared the liver out of me but I'm still alive and very lucky to be that way. Listen, Jeff, does Grace know about me?"

"Oh, yes, she knows all about you."

"Did she phone you? She's not worried about me, is she?"

There was a pause during which the telephone lines strung between us hummed and crackled and cleared their throats.

"Jeff?"

"Yes, Ellen Grae, I'm still here."

"Did Grace phone you? What did she say?"

Jeff's voice, suddenly loud and clear and very strong, filled my ear. It said, "Yes, your mother phoned. As a matter of fact she's phoned three times since noon today."

"I hope she's not worried about me. What did she say?"

Came Jeff's answer, an orderly, sorrowful knell. "She said that she was disappointed in you and I might add so am I. She said she had never thought she would live to see the day when our daughter would resort to trickery and I might add that this is also precisely my own sentiment. Do you understand me, Ellen Grae?"

"Yes, sir, I understand you."

"Then," said Jeff, "I'm going to say good-bye for now and hang up. I suggest that you write to us in a few days and let us know how you feel about things."

"Yes, sir, I will."

"Good-bye then, for now."

"Good-bye, sir."

The fat lady's stomach, filled with chocolate creams, liverwurst, bread, cake, cheese, crackers, an eclair, and three soda pops, gurgled in its sodden sleep. I forced myself to look away from its enormous bulk.

Chapter 11

THERE WAS THIS TIME of inner turmoil, several days of it, and I reckon some of it seeped through to the surface and made people sorry for me. Their looks commiserated, they laughed at my jokes even when they weren't funny, they tagged after me even to the bathroom.

"If you think I sneaked in here to cut my throat you're mistaken," I said to Laura. "I'm just looking for some aspirin. How come you're up so early?"

Attired in long pants, a thick sweat shirt, and sneakers Laura went to the window and flung it open with such energy that the panes rattled. "We're going clam digging," she announced. "All of us. Smith Smith and Victoria, too. You haven't got a headache, have you?"

"Oh, no. No, I'm just gulping this aspirin in case I *do* get one. Where are we going to dig for clams?"

A wispy clot of six-o'clock fog drifted in through the open window and settled like a halo on Laura's mahogany curls. Her grin reminded me of Grover's. "I dunno. Some beach, I guess. What's the difference? Come on, let's go."

Aunt Eleanor and Assunta, both of them dressed like Laura, were waiting for us in the kitchen. A party mood pervaded. We rushed through toast and hot chocolate and then out to the car, the back of which was filled with two hampers of food, pails, four narrow shovels otherwise known as clam guns, Smith Smith The Seventh, and Victoria.

Solemn as hoot owls the Smiths inquired after everyone's health, pointed out the assets of the day, apologized for knowing where to go to dig the best and biggest clams, and Victoria settled back into anticipatory silence. Smith Smith shared his scholarly knowledge of the geoduc clam—the kind we were going after: "I've found three ways to spell it," he said. "G e o d u c, g w e d u c, and g e o d u c k. We prounce it gooeyduck. It is the largest burrowing clam in the world."

Laura climbed in to sit beside me, Assunta took her rightful place in the passenger's side of the front seat, Aunt Eleanor took a cheerful check of heads and provisions, jumped in, slammed the door, tested the horn a couple of times to make sure it was working, turned the ignition key, heavily pressed the gas pedal with her foot, and we shot out of the driveway and down in to the street.

A bare-boned dog appeared on the opposite curb and viewed our passing with alarm.

Assunta rolled down the window on her side and cold, fresh air rushed in.

Smith Smith The Seventh and Victoria turned their collars up and drew closer to each other.

At this hour Seattle and all that surrounds it is a powerful dose. The color and smell of everything is clear and sharp. The city is fresh. Outlying lakes appear unspoiled. Beaches are long, rippled stretches of tan silk. When we reached the one where Smith Smith and Victoria said geoducs were to be found Aunt Eleanor screeched the car to a halt and Assunta commanded everybody to pile out and start working whether they felt like it or not.

Laura and Smith Smith and Victoria and I ran around collecting driftwood and Assunta and Aunt Eleanor built a fire. I thought we'd be allowed to get warm by it but Assunta and Aunt Eleanor were the only ones who settled down before its blaze. Assunta pointed to the shovels and said, "Clams. That's what we came out here for. Don't get any wetter than you have to. Better take the pails along. Come back when they're full. Have fun."

Digging a geoduc out of his semipermanent burrow is not fun—it's work.

Smith Smith instructed us. "You won't find him on the surface. He'll be buried a couple or three feet beneath the sand. Watch out for bubbles. Geoducs have long siphons which they send upward through the sand. When they're disturbed they retract their siphons expelling contained water as they do and this action causes bubbles. When you find one don't try to pull him out by his siphon—it'll break off. Holler for the rest of us and we'll dig him out whole."

Victoria was the first to locate one. It took almost an hour to dig him out. It had a long, thick, ivory colored neck and its body, partially enclosed between two dirty-white shells that resembled wings, was as large as a hen's. Smith Smith said he'd weigh at least five pounds.

Laura touched his bulbous body with her finger and with a tinge of wistfulness said, "I wish Grover could be here to see him."

Upon the instruction of Smith Smith I filled the bottom of a pail with sea water, we dumped the geoduc in it and moved on down the beach.

The sun came out and warmed us.

We met a man who looked like an Eskimo who told us in flawless English that he also was a would-be gooeyducker. Smith Smith invited him to join us but he declined and strode away, a sparse, lonely figure.

"He looked like an Eskimo," I said. "Was he?"

"It's possible," replied Smith Smith, with a dry, unimaginative look.

"One of my best friends is an Eskimo," I said. "Her name is Yuki. That means snow in Japanese."

"We know," apologized Victoria. "We used to live in Japan."

"Oh. Oh, yes, that's right you did, didn't you? I forgot about that."

Laura left Victoria's side and came over to walk

along beside me. She said, "I remember Yuki, Ellen Grae."

I turned my head and looked into her face. Her eyes had taken on an astonishing color. They were brown, like Grover's. Her bones beneath the smooth, fine-textured skin that covered them, suddenly looked like his, too. Very bony.

I said, "You remember Yuki, Laura? That's funny."

"Yuki," said Laura, testing the word and drawing Smith Smith and Victoria into soft, infatuated confidence. "She worked for the Royal Canadian Mounties. The Canadian Mounted Police some people call them. When's the last time you heard from her, Ellen Grae?"

"Oh, about six months, I reckon."

The Smiths craned their necks and gazed at me, their khaki-colored eyespots oddly flickering. As one they said, "We didn't know that Royal Canadian Mounted Police hired women."

"They don't," I said. "But Yuki knows how to build igloos and cook blubber and harpoon seals and can tell, just by putting her ear to the ground when the icebergs are getting ready to crack up and start moving around so they hired her as a kind of scout. She knows how to train sled dogs, too."

"Huk, huk!" whooped Laura, letting the mood of the story take full possession. "Go, go! Go, dog, go! Remember, Ellen Grae?"

"Yes. Huk, huk! And the polar foxes running back and forth ahead of our sleds—"

"—and the ice cracking up all around us, heaving and thundering in all that polar silence—"

Laura raised a shaking hand to her mouth. "Tell them about the iceberg, Ellen Grae," she whispered.

"Oh, yes. Crimenitti, that iceberg, I'll never forget it! We were stranded on it. We thought it was ground covered with snow and hoarfrost and pitched our camp on it but in the middle of the night the ocean beneath us began to move and swell. I was the first one to wake up and jump up and look out but all I could see for miles and miles all around were big ice floes crumbling and tilting and straining. There was this ghostly haze shining over everything and the fearful force of the sea beneath us raging. I sounded the alarm and everybody quick got up and grabbed what clothes they could. I grabbed a box of pemmican—that's dried meat and blubber ground up—but that's all we were able to save. The iceberg with us on top of it slowly, slowly moved out to the Bering Sea."

Laura put her hand on her stomach, the same way Grover does sometimes, and breathed.

Smith Smith put his arm around Victoria. The spots in her eyes had all blurred and run together. She shivered.

"We lost everything—our dogs, our sleds, all of my father's painting stuff, our clothes, and our food. Everything. For two days and two nights we were stranded on top of that iceberg. My father painted a picture of it when we got back home showing Mount McKinley on one side and Russia on the other and a lot of other icebergs floating around in between, crunching against each other. The aurora borealis came out and lighted up the whole sky and it was really pretty but we didn't look at it much because we were so cold and scared and hungry. Some planes flew over and we sent up flares and desperately prayed for them to turn and come back and rescue us but they didn't. Well, so we didn't think we'd ever be rescued and resigned ourselves but on the third day this beautiful Eskimo girl named Yuki came in her canoe and got us off the iceberg and took us back to her Eskimo camp. We were frozen stiff as boards and our stomachs had shrunk up to the size of walnuts but Yuki's father went out and killed three polar bears and made us each a fur coat and some mukluks from sealskin. Yuki made us blood pudding from the polar bears' livers. It didn't taste too good but it was real nourishing."

Smith Smith shifted the pail containing the geoduc

from one hand to the other. He said, "I think icebergs are interesting."

We searched and searched but didn't find any more geoducs.

For lunch we had roasting ears dripping with butter and salmon salad sandwiches on big, homemade buns.

On the way home Aunt Eleanor drove by the school which Laura and I would attend in the coming term. Every brick and flower was in place. It looked democratic.

Comes a rising of the spirit at the end of such a day. In the evening the music from Smith Smith The Seventh's harp filled the quiet air and afterward the night settled down and so did we. Aunt Eleanor came as she always did to say good-night. She said for me to look under my bed if I had any trouble going to sleep and I looked and there was a pile of books.

I lay in my comfortable bed and thought about this new life that had been created for me. I thought about Thicket and the letters I would write to Jeff and Grace and in this reverie I saw myself standing on a new hygienic shore. Then there surged in me an increase in reason and understanding and my obligations to what I had been fell away and were replaced with a new indebtedness to what I was.

I was at peace with myself and the world but unbeknownst to me there were forces at work which were not to allow me to stay and enjoy that which I had mastered.

I can only suppose that my letters to Grace and Jeff had something to do with it. I was very careful to be truthful and to set down exactly what I felt and thought. Aunt Eleanor said that they were very wholesome and moving.

Anyway, forty-eight hours later a new set of orders came from Thicket. Aunt Eleanor, distressed and a little angry, delivered them. "Now they want

you to come home," she declared, waving two type-
written sheets. "I don't understand it. I wish they'd
make up their minds. Who on earth is Irby Fudge?"

"He's the sheriff in Thicket."

"The sheriff? I don't understand. What on earth
does the sheriff in Thicket have to do with you?"

"Nothing. I just know him."

"Are you friends?"

"Oh, sure. Everybody in Thicket is friends with
everybody else. Are you sure Jeff and Grace want me
to come home now? I don't understand it either. First
they want me to come up here. Then they want me
to come back. I swear. What's that pink slip? A note
for me?"

Aunt Eleanor rattled the sheets and waved the slip.
"It's a check for your plane fare. They don't want
you to get off in Chicago. Did Mr. McGruder give you
a valuable coin of some kind, Ellen Grae?"

"He gave me a Maria Theresa dollar. I don't know
how valuable it is. You want to see it?"

Aunt Eleanor rattled the sheets some more. "No.
He'll want to though. He wants you to bring it back
to him, deliver it to him in person. Grover wants you
to bring him a geoduc. The egg man and lady want
you to come and see their babies. The caretaker at the
cemetery wants you to come and look at some new
headstones that have been added. What on earth for?"

"Oh, he knows I like headstones. Grover and I go
out there sometimes just to look around."

Aunt Eleanor chewed some of her lipstick off. "I'm
a little provoked with Jeff and Grace. I don't understand their thinking. I thought we were all settled. I
don't know what they think can be gained by making
this second move. You're happy here now, aren't
you?"

"Yes, ma'am, I certainly am. I'm all adjusted. But if
they want me to come back I reckon I'll have to go.
I'm sorry for all the trouble I've been to you, Aunt
Eleanor."

Aunt Eleanor looked at me and the anger went out

of her face. "You haven't been any trouble to me, honey." She said, "Well, I suppose we'd better make some plans. I'd better call the airport. Is your little checked suit clean, Ellen Grae?"

"Oh, yes, ma'am, it's spotless. I've been very careful with it."

This was an inadvertent lie; the suit's jacket had a mustard spot on its sleeve but Assunta cleaned it off for me. In return for this favor she said she wouldn't mind having the jar containing the Thicket dirt. Secretly I don't think she really wanted it, I think she was just afraid that it would spill during my journey. But I gave it to her.

Chapter 12

THICKET HADN'T CHANGED ANY. When I got off the train and breathed in its torpid heat and smelled its dry, elusive scent and looked around at all the buildings, leaning against each other in tired, gingerbread array, I said that to Jeff and Grover. "It hasn't changed a bit," I said. "Now it seems so small. Seattle is huge, you know. It's so beautiful, all walled in by mountains and water. So beautiful. My, it's hot. In Seattle it was very cool when I left."

"If your hands are hot you could take off your gloves," Grover suggested, sliding his amber eyes around.

"Don't be gauche, Grover. A lady never goes out in public with bare hands. That's *one* of the things I learned in Seattle, thank heaven."

Grover stuck his hand inside his shirt and softly scratched.

Jeff stowed my bags in the trunk of the car, came around and got in it and we drove home. Under a smelting, noonday sun the neighborhood streets were quiet. We passed the McGruders' house and Jeff glanced at me, I think expecting me to lean out and holler but I didn't.

I felt queerly humbled and subdued.

"Your mother will be here tomorrow," said Jeff. "She's going to stay with the McGruders."

My cup ran over.

This homecoming was the nicest day I had ever experienced. Grover had lunch with Jeff and me but didn't bolt his food like he usually did. I only had to remind him once to use his napkin. Afterward he solemnly thanked me for the present I'd brought him —a gooeyduck packed in dry ice. "Boy," he said, examining the clam's long, ivory neck. "Boy. This here's a real specimen. I'm going to take him home right now and show him to my uncle. Boy, Ellen Grae, you sure were nice to think to bring him to me. I sure thank you."

I told him the truth; that the geoduc wasn't actually a present from me. "Smith Smith The Seventh and his sister Victoria sent him to you. When I write to them you can enclose a little thank-you note if you want."

Hugging the sack that contained the geoduc and the dry ice Grover edged toward the door. With a pensive expression in his eyes he said, "I don't suppose you want to go down to the river after a while and look around."

"Oh, I wouldn't mind, Grover. After I have a talk with Jeff I wouldn't mind."

He said, "Your head still doesn't look natural. It's still got red and green spots."

I said, "Yours would have red and green spots, too, if it had been put to the strenuous use mine had."

For the first time that day Grover grinned. "Yeah,"

he said. "Yeah." And, lugging his prize, he went home.

Jeff and I sat in the kitchen where there was a little breeze and drank two glasses of iced tea each and had a little talk. I told him truthfully that I was sorry for all the trouble I had caused and was even more sorry that I had had to come back from Seattle before I learned any big, new values.

Jeff said, "Well, maybe the time wasn't right."

"Seattle is a beautiful city," I said. "It's a wonder to me more people don't know about it. And in between there is certainly a lot of large country. My, I never saw so much land and so many people. Jeff, did you ever notice that I have an accent?"

Jeff finished the last of his tea. "Yes, I've noticed."

"In Seattle they don't have any accents. They speak pure American. I'm going to try and improve mine. I never realized how ignorant I sounded until I went out there and listened to those people talk. And another thing—when they get up in the mornings they don't slop around like we do down here. They put on clothes and keep them on all day. Oh, I want to tell you about the Seattle Art Museum. It has a permanent collection of Chinese jade that's centuries and centuries old. It must be worth billions of dollars. And their contemporary art is . . . Jeff, you know what I was thinking coming back on the plane?"

There was bright quicksilver in Jeff's eyes. He shook his head.

"I was thinking that I might be destined to become an artist like you. When we were flying over Illinois I thought that. All that wheat which people down here don't even know about. Or was it soybeans? Well, anyway, the fields were just lovely. Have you ever seen a painting of a wheat field or a soybean one? Oh, that reminds me. I want to look up about soybeans. And earthquakes. Jeff, do you know what the Richter scale is?"

Jeff nodded. The quicksilver in his eyes was bubbling.

"It's funny that I didn't know what it was until I went to Seattle and was in that earthquake. Oh, heck, there's so much I don't know about. I'm ignorant, did you know that? I hate to admit it but I'm just plain old ignorant. I swear. If that doesn't beat all. I'm kind of disgusted with myself."

Jeff said, "Well, don't let it throw you. Look on the optimistic side."

"What optimistic side? There isn't any optimistic side to ignorance. I hate it when I don't know things."

Jeff said, "That's the optimistic side. Before something can be done about ignorance it must first be recognized. You just think that over for a while and then let me know what you think about it."

"All right, sir. I will. I surely will. But, Jeff, before I start on that I want you to settle something in my mind for me, if you will. You don't have to answer me if you don't want to; if it's supposed to be kept between you and Grace. But what I want to know is: Why am I home?"

Something in Jeff's face flickered. He breathed one short breath and two long ones. He turned in his chair and showed me his profile. He said, "Well, in the first place this is where you belong, Ellen Grae."

"Yes, sir, I know that. I've always known that. But I mean why am I here *now?* Why did you and Grace have me come back from Seattle?"

Jeff rubbed the back of his neck with his hand and breathed two more times. He said, "Well, I'll tell you, Ellen Grae. It's like this. You and Grace and I are a family. Right?"

"Right."

"We don't live together but that doesn't make any difference. We're still a family. Right?"

"Right."

"And families, the members of them, should be close to one another. It's bad enough to be separated as we are. With you one place during school terms and Grace another and me another but at least up until the time we sent you to Seattle we were all in the same state. You understand me, Ellen Grae?"

"Yes, sir, but—"

"So that's why we had you come back," continued Jeff, breathing again. "So we could all at least be in the same state together. You aren't going to be a child forever, Ellen Grae."

"No, sir, I know that."

"And life is precarious," said Jeff.

"Yes, sir, it surely is. Life is very precarious."

Jeff turned his head and smiled at me.

It was satisfying to be home. As soon as Jeff left to do a downtown errand I unpacked all my stuff, putting everything where it belonged—my dresses on hangers, my shoes on the shoe rack in the closet, my books under my bed. I hurried.

About one o'clock Grover came back. He looked at my pants and paint-spattered shirt and said, "Well, I see you're back in uniform."

"Don't be facetious, Grover. I'm only wearing these old clothes because I have to save my good ones for school. Jeff and Grace aren't rich. They can't go out and buy me new clothes every week. What did you do with the gooeyduck?"

"Put him in the refrigerator. I weighed him first. You know how much he weighed?"

"Yes, Grover. I lugged him all the way from Seattle, remember? Are you ready to go or are we just going to stand around here all day?"

Grover said he was ready to go and we set out. For once he didn't ask me to carry anything, not even the hoe.

As old as my memory, the field, crackling dry, thick with erupting clouds of black gnats, and the tawny river, still darkly flowing, greeted us. Two pot-bellied birds, one with juvenal plumage, whistled combatively from the opposite bank. Grover flapped his arms and whistled back and they pedaled themselves up and disappeared into the cool swamp bower.

"Dumb birds," said Grover. "Dumb old birds."

In my absence the boat had received a new coat of paint—orange on the inside and green on the out. It looked kind of garish but I didn't say anything. It wasn't a day for criticism.

For once Grover didn't remind me that it was my job to shove us off. He did it and smoothly we moved out into the middle of the stream. The two birds returned to watch our departure.

"Which way do you want to go?" asked Grover. "Upstream or down?"

"I don't care."

"You want to fish?"

"I don't care."

"Or would you just rather drift around and look at things?"

"I don't care."

Grover pushed his white captain's cap to the back of his head. "Ellen Grae, I thought of a new way to make money while you were gone."

"That's nice."

"You know what epiphytes are?"

"Sure, sure."

"Epiphytes are those air plants you see growing wild out there. Mrs. Merriweather is crazy about them. She said she'd give us a quarter apiece for every good one we brought to her."

"Who's Mrs. Merriweather?"

"You know. The lady who runs the nursery."

"Oh, yeah. Well, I'll tell you, Grover. I'm not much interested in money today. I've been in a push and a shove ever since summer started and I'm tired. Before anything else happens I'm going to rest a while."

Off our bow a big, snub-nosed catfish dimpled the water's surface. Grover just looked at him. "I'm tired too. I worked hard while you were gone. Every danged animal in the country decided to be sick and they all decided to do it at the same time. They kept my uncle and me runnin' twenty-four hours a day. It clean tuckered me, I swear it did."

"Don't gripe, Grover. Let's not gripe about anything today. Look at this primeval world out here. Isn't it beautiful?"

Grover grinned. "Yeah, beautiful. I like it. How does your head feel?"

"Almost normal again."

Grover hooked one leg around his idle pole. "I wrote a poem about you just now. Want to hear it?"

"A poem. Oh, sure, Grover. Sure I want to hear it."

Grover put two fingers inside his shirt and scratched. He sucked his cheeks and wiggled his bare toes. He said:

> "ELLEN GRAE USED HER HEAD
>   TO GET A TICKET.
>   NOW IT'S ALL GREEN AND RED
>   BUT SHE'S BACK IN THICKET."

An insect with black, transparent wings and a yellow stomach landed on my arm. I brushed it away.

Beneath us the river whispered.

About the Authors

When he was five, Bill Cleaver's parents were divorced and he and his brother were sent by his father, a Seattle, Washington, attorney, to private school at Vancouver Island, British Columbia, for their education. At seventeen, Bill left school and joined first the U.S. Navy and then the Merchant Marine. During WWII he was crew member of a B-24 bomber, serving in the U.S. Air Corps in the European Theater of Operations. In 1945 he returned to the States and he and Vera Cleaver were married.

Vera Cleaver is the fifth of nine children. She was born in Virgil, South Dakota, and began her schooling in Kennebec, South Dakota. Her father was traveling auditor for a western railroad and made frequent moves with the family to Nebraska, Wyoming, and finally north Florida. Vera and Bill Cleaver have lived in Washington State, California, and North Carolina, as well as in France and Japan. Their home presently is in Winter Haven, Florida.

The Cleavers did not begin writing seriously until some years after they married, but after starting with short stories and then books for young people, they won recognition quickly. Three of their novels have been nominated for National Book Awards, and one, *Where the Lilies Bloom*, became an acclaimed major film.

The Cleavers share a love for the music of old masters, horticulture, antiques, old countrysides, bird-watching, bird-befriending, animal-befriending, and libraries.

SIGNET Books by Phyllis A. Whitney

☐	CREOLE HOLIDAY	(#W8224—$1.50)
☐	THE HIGHEST DREAM	(#Y6552—$1.25)
☐	LINDA'S HOMECOMING	(#W9004—$1.50)
☐	A LONG TIME COMING	(#W9310—$1.50)
☐	MYSTERY OF THE ANGRY IDOL	(#Y8435—$1.25)
☐	MYSTERY OF THE BLACK DIAMONDS	(#W8612—$1.50)
☐	MYSTERY OF THE GOLDEN HORN	(#Y8029—$1.25)
☐	MYSTERY OF THE GULLS	(#Y7798—$1.25)
☐	MYSTERY OF THE HIDDEN HAND	(#W9028—$1.50)
☐	MYSTERY OF THE SCOWLING BOY	(#Y7530—$1.25)
☐	MYSTERY OF THE STRANGE TRAVELER	(#E9847—$1.75)
☐	MYSTERY ON THE ISLE OF SKYE	(#W9151—$1.50)
☐	NOBODY LIKES TRINA	(#W8275—$1.50)
☐	SECRET OF GOBLIN GLEN	(#Y7420—$1.25)
☐	SECRET OF THE HAUNTED MESA	(#Y7913—$1.25)
☐	SECRET OF THE SAMURAI SWORD	(#W9155—$1.50)
☐	SECRET OF THE SPOTTED SHELL	(#Y7468—$1.25)
☐	SECRET OF THE TIGER'S EYE	(#W8298—$1.50)*
☐	STEP TO THE MUSIC	(#W7531—$1.50)

* Price slightly higher in Canada

Buy them at your local
bookstore or use coupon
on next page for ordering.

MS READ-a-thon—
a simple way to start
youngsters reading

Boys and girls between 6 and 14 can join the MS READ-a-thon and help find a cure for Multiple Sclerosis by reading books. And they get two rewards — the enjoyment of reading, and the great feeling that comes from helping others.

Parents and educators: For complete information call your local MS chapter. Or mail the coupon below.

Kids can help, too!

Hoping for conclusion I went back up to the